The Rise of Magic

Phil Brown

More instalments of the Windwicche Stables

series will be available in 2024

ISBN-13: 9798867341305

For Angela and Stanley

1

The Worst Day Ever

I knew it was bad when I heard the siren.

'It's behind us John, pull over.' Mum was peering round from the front seat of our old Volvo, looking past me and Freya to see out of the rear window.

Dad grumbled under his breath, then braked and turned the steering wheel, making the car go wonky and butt into the kerb.

Wooooo-waaah, Wooooo-waaah ...

The high side of a big vehicle roared past us, blue lights glaring in the dusk.

'That's a fire engine,' Mum said. Like we hadn't all just seen it go by.

'Where's it going?' Freya, my little sister, asked from the seat next to me.

A cold weight in my tummy told me where it was going. I glanced down at my phone, at the message I'd read over and over, and that had made me beg mum and dad until they bundled us into the car and drove out into the early evening darkness.

Pls come down - really need your help - now 🙏

Dad spun the steering wheel and then we were moving again. I could still see the flashing blue lights ahead of us, getting smaller in the distance.

Please just keep going... please.

Mum gasped. 'It's turning down the lane to the stables.'

Dad muttered a swearword.

'John!' Mum told him off.

Our indicator ticked and dad turned us into the lane. And there it was again, the fire engine with its strobing blue lights, going slower now, dipping and lurching as its wheels found the potholes in the lane's rough surface. Then its big red brake lights flared and it turned again, going left into the stables' car park.

We bumped along behind, Dad twisting the steering wheel from side to side to avoid spindly branches that grasped out from the trees on either side.

Then we were there and we turned into the car park and Freya squeaked. 'No!'

Mum breathed another word that we weren't meant to know.

Flames were leaping high into the evening sky, making everything else dark and hard to see; the fire engine was just a huge blocky shape, and there were people standing next to it that looked like shadow puppets.

Dad pulled the car to a stop and I scrabbled to find the doorhandle.

Click!

The door fell open and I stumbled out and started running, smells like firework-night tickling inside my nose and wafts of hot air warming my cheeks.

Someone called my name. 'Poppy!'

Was that Chloe?

One of the puppet shapes waved its arms and ran towards me. We bumped and crashed, arms entangled around each other, nearly falling into the mud and puddles.

'What have we done?' Chloe sobbed.

2

The Best Day Ever

FIVE WEEKS EARLIER...

'You'll love it.' Mum was using her pretend-optimistic voice.

'I won't'.

'I did at your age.'

'Back in prehistoric times.'

'You can't just hang around the house all summer.'

No point in answering that one. Before I knew it, I'd be banned from my laptop, and from my phone, and she'd expect me to spend all the holidays just reading or something.

'Anyway, it'll help you make friends.'

And that's what this was really all about. Guilt. Mum and dad had just moved us from one end of the country to the other and, what a surprise, me and Freya don't have any friends here. Freya's only little so she doesn't care so much. But I'm thirteen. My friends are all still on Snapchat – I'm just never going to see them again.

Turn right down Windwicche Lane.

I gave the satnav a glare, like this was all its fault. It showed a road coming up that looked tiny. Hardly a road at all. That figured, where we were going just *had* to be in the middle of nowhere.

Mum took the turn and... Oh my god! The road was really bad. It was overgrown at the sides by trees and bushes, and interlaced branches overhead cut out the early morning sunshine and made it like a gloomy tunnel. It hardly seemed wide enough to drive down, and its surface was made of stones and mud and puddles. God help us if anything came the other way.

Mum twisted the steering wheel right and left to avoid the deeper holes and the car bumped and jerked and splashed as it went along.

'Gosh Mum,' I muttered. 'I hope the car doesn't get dirty or scratched or anything.'

She flashed me a glance and after a moment she laughed. 'Funn...y.'

And suddenly I was laughing too.

Mum was annoying like that. I could never stay cross with her for long.

'Welcome to Windwicche stables!' The short round lady in front of us was so full of smiley-ness I thought she might burst. 'I hope you enjoy your time here.'

My time? That sounded like a prison sentence. Which it kind of was.

The lady had stopped talking and seemed to be waiting for something from me... like a smile, or some words, or god knows what. Not a chance. I just stared over her shoulder.

Mum butted in with her embarrassed voice. 'She's a bit shy...'

Shy? Actually, *she* was a bit hacked off.

Mum kept going. 'We've only just moved to the area and she doesn't have any friends here.'

Oh yeah, thanks a lot, make me sound like a loser.

I glanced around. Beyond the fence at the edge of the carpark was a big overgrown garden with a ratty-looking bungalow in the middle of it. And down at the bottom of the car park a path led away between two big bushes. Based on the smells coming up from that direction, that had to be where the horses lived.

A tall girl about my age was clanking past us with a dirty pink wheelbarrow, overflowing with brown-smeared yellow grassy stuff. She must've heard what mum just said, because she snorted a laugh and made a goofy face at me as she went by.

'At least I don't smell like poo,' I muttered at her back.

If she heard, she ignored me, and just carried on towards a gap in the fence on the far side of the car park.

'I'm sure you'll soon make friends here,' the smiley lady kept on talking.

'Well,' mum made a big thing of looking at her phone to check the time. 'I hope you don't mind, but I need to get back to start work.'

The lady said no problem and waved her away, and in moments mum was back in the car, turning it around, and bumping and jolting away.

And that was me... dumped!

'I expect you want a cup of tea,' the round lady said, and led the way down towards the path at the end of the carpark.

I actually didn't, but then there were lots of things I didn't want, like being here in the first place. So I kept quiet and followed her anyway.

It turned out the path did lead to where the horses lived. It opened out onto an expanse of dirty-looking concrete with long, low buildings running down each side. Horses' heads poked out of the opened-up tops of stable doors. They all swivelled round to look at us.

The lady laughed at them. 'They want their breakfast.'

I tried to walk around the puddles in the cracked concrete but somehow brown stuff still splashed up onto my Ugg Ultras. I hoped it was just mud.

There were more girls in the yard, all rushing around and doing something; heaving nets of dried grass, pushing wheelbarrows, leading horses around, carrying buckets. Some were about my age, but there were younger ones too, and one girl who looked much older. We passed a little girl who was only about eight, leading a short, fat pony through the yard.

'Hello'. She peered at me through thick glasses. 'This is Bella, I'm having a lesson on her later.'

Bella was cute. Deep brown with shaggy hair down the back of her neck. Her dark eyes looked up at me and her whole face was like a cheeky grin.

'You can stroke her if you want.'

'No...'

The girl ran her hand up and down the pony's nose. 'She likes it like this.'

I gave in and reached my hand out. Bella's fur was rough and scratchy. The pony let me stroke her a couple of times before she tossed her head suddenly.

The girl giggled as I jumped back. 'She doesn't mean it... she likes you really.'

'Are you sure?'

'Yeah, she didn't bite you.'

A shout made me look up. 'Come on, Poppy. This way!'

The round lady had got ahead of me. She was beckoning for me to follow her through a wide gap between the stable buildings on the right-hand side of the yard.

I gave the girl a sorry-gotta-go look.

The other side of the gap was a big rectangular space with fences all around and a wide gate at the front. The ground inside was made of sandy, muddy stuff.

'That's our menage.' The lady said, as she turned right just before the gate and sidled along a narrow pathway squashed between the outside of the menage fence and a ratty wooden shed. About halfway along the shed's wall a door was hanging open.

Inside the shed was bigger than it looked.

There was a dusty sofa against one wall with a low table in front of it which was littered with unwashed mugs, most of them cracked and chipped with cutesy messages on them; like 'Dad's Tea', and 'I went to Margate and all I got was this stupid mug', and 'Comic Relief 2018'...

'Sorry, no one ever seems to wash up,' the lady muttered.

I had to look away, the mugs were disgusting.

The lady clicked the switch on an electric kettle perched at the end of a long bench against the wall opposite the sofa. Above the bench was a long row of windows, with dirty glass and spiders living in the corners, but which... I let out a tiny 'wow'... gave an amazing view of the menage outside. I watched someone ride a horse out into the middle.

The noise of the kettle boiling pulled my gaze back into the shed, and I saw the round lady poised with teabags hovering over two mugs that didn't look much cleaner than the ones down on the table.

'Uh... maybe I won't have tea,' I tried.

'Nonsense, you'll need something to keep you going.'

The only other furniture in the room was a desk back near the door with three rickety chairs in front of it and an office chair behind. On the desk a computer looked so old and grubby I couldn't believe it still worked.

The lady sat me in one of the chairs at the front of the desk, while she plumped down in the office chair behind.

I stared at the mug of milky tea in front of me.

Then tried a sip.

Yuck!

It was weak and sugary. And the cracked mug randomly stated it was 'Paul's Tea'.

'Drink up, Poppy, then Allie will show you the ropes,' the round lady said.

A girl rushed past the windows outside and stumped in through the door. 'Bev said you wanted me.'

Oh god! It was that girl who had the pink wheelbarrow.

'Yes, can you show Poppy how to muck out?'

The girl glanced down at me, taking in my light blue 501's and white North Face T, not to mention the already-brown-flecked Uggs.

She flashed me a sarky smile. 'Yeah... it'll be a pleasure.'

Mucking out turned out to be exactly what it sounded like.

Allie found me a rusty, old wheelbarrow and took me down to the end of the yard. There was a row of five stables there that looked better than the others. They were nearly twice as big, with freshly varnished doors and hinges black and shiny with new paint.

'These're the liveries,' Allie announced, without explaining what she meant. She parked the wheelbarrow next to the stable on the right-hand end then hauled on the bolts to open the top and bottom doors. I peered in. Yellowy, thick grassy stuff was piled high on the floor.

'Where's the horse?' I managed, at the same time as gagging on the smell that had just invaded my nostrils.

'All the liveries are out in the paddocks.'

She went in and used a fork to rake the yellow stuff from side to side.

'What you gotta do is... separate out the dirty straw and put it in the 'barrow, and when that's done pile the clean straw that's left around the edges so the floor can dry out.'

She got a forkful of straw with a pile of horse poo on top and heaved it into the wheelbarrow.

'You try.'

She shoved the fork at me, and I managed to grab it before it touched the leg of my jeans.

I gave her a look and she shrugged. 'Good luck staying clean.'

I edged past her into the stable.

Why was I even going along with this?

I pushed the fork into the straw and pulled some towards me. Yuck, definitely dirty. I heaved it up and took it out of the door and dumped it on top of the forkful that was already in the wheelbarrow.

'Okay. You got it. S'not rocket science. When the 'barrow's full, empty it on the dung heap next to the carpark.'

'Sir, yes sir!' In my best US-marine voice.

She gave me a twisted don't-be-stupid smile. 'Just get all these liveries done by lunchtime.'

Then she turned and walked away.

That Allie girl might be an idiot, but she was right about keeping clean.

It was impossible.

It was also going to be impossible to get all the livery stables done in just one morning.

But I kept on going – forking dirty straw into the wheelbarrow – then traipsing up the yard to the muck heap to empty it – then going back down to start forking again.

On my fourth run back down to the stables something made me stop in mid-stride – a loud sob.

Who was that? I parked the wheelbarrow in the middle of the yard and followed the sad noise to one of the stables.

I looked over the open top door and saw Bella, the little pony I'd stroked in the yard earlier. She looked as happy and mischievous as ever, but the little girl had her face buried in the thatch of shaggy hair running down the back of her neck.

She was sobbing and sobbing and sobbing.

'What's so bad?' I asked.

The girl looked up, her glasses crooked and about to fall off her face. She had a black helmet-thing on her head. Huh? In my memory she'd been wearing a hat with bright yellow and green stripes. But then I saw a sad spill of silky material on the stable floor and realised it must be some sort of cover for her helmet.

'You should get that before it's messed up,' I said.

'Oh yeah,' the girl sniffed, and scooped it up from the floor. 'I got it for my birthday.'

She clenched it in her hands and leaned her head back on her pony.

'So, what's wrong?' I tried again.

'It's not Bella's fault.'

'What isn't?'

'I'm just no good.'

'No good at what?'

'Anything... I can't even canter.'

Canter? Wasn't that when a horse ran along?

'Well, it sounds very hard.'

'Everyone can canter.'

I shrugged. 'I can't. I've never ridden at all. So, you're better than me.'

The girl looked up and took a moment to straighten up her glasses and stare.

'Never?'

'Nope, never.'

'Why'd you come here then?'

'My mum,' I made a you-know-what-mums-are-like face. 'She wants me out of the house for the summer holidays... and *she* loved riding when *she* was young.'

'Oh... well, maybe me and Bella could teach you,' the girl said, swiping at her cheeks. 'At least how to walk, and maybe trot.'

I held up a not-so-fast hand. 'Just don't make me do any cantering.'

She gave a long sniff. 'Okay.'

'Good,' I got out my phone and glanced at it. Nearly 11am. 'But I can't do it now, I've got to get all the liveries mucked out by lunchtime, whenever that is.'

The girl's mouth opened in shock. 'On your own?'

'That's what they told me.'

'I'll come and help.'

'Really?'

'Yeah.'

'Okay.'

'I just have to un-tack Bella first.'

I smiled and headed back to my wheelbarrow. That little girl was nice. I didn't know how much help she was going to be. She wasn't very big, even for her age. But it was good of her to offer.

It turned out the little girl was way better than me at mucking out.

When she came down and found me, she told me her name was Kate.

'Like the princess?' I asked, which had made her giggle.

Then I told her I was Poppy, and she said it
nice name.

She was so sweet and so innocent... how did she
ever get on with the other girls here?

All morning I'd seen Allie laughing in huddles with
her friends, then going quiet whenever I went past
with my wheelbarrow, with god-knows-what streaked
across my jeans and my T shirt, and my Uggs
completely covered in... whatever. The whole lot
would only be fit for binning when I got home.

Finally, Kate and me finished the last livery stable
and I looked at my phone.

13.12.

I had no idea whether that meant we'd finished on
time, or even if the lunchtime deadline was just
something Allie had made up.

But I did know that it would've taken me all day on
my own. And the other thing I knew was that I was
starving.

'Is there any way to get something to eat here?' I
asked Kate as we took the last wheelbarrow-load
through the car park.

The little girl shrugged like she didn't know. 'My
mum comes to get me at lunchtime.'

'How come?'

Kate looked down at the ground. 'Some of them aren't nice to me if I stay and eat here.'

Some of them? I kind of knew who she meant.

Then someone called out. 'Kate, are you ready?'

I looked up and saw a grown-up lady who looked a bit like Kate walking towards us. 'That has to be your mum.'

Kate cheered up instantly. 'Yeah – come and meet her.'

I didn't know if I wanted to. But Kate had already run over to the lady and so I set down the wheelbarrow and followed her.

'Mum. This is Poppy. She's nice.'

The lady smiled at me, a happy smile, but with something in it that was sad too. 'Thank you.'

'What for?'

'Being nice to Kate.'

I shrugged. 'She's sweet.'

The lady nodded. 'She is.'

The lady crouched down and looked into Kate's face. 'How did it go today with Bella?'

Kate's smile dropped. 'Not so good.' But she didn't start crying again.

'Never mind.' The lady stood up again. 'Ready to go?'

Kate nodded and grabbed her hand and then they were walking away towards a silver car near the car park entrance. As Kate got in the passenger side she waved and called out. 'See you tomorrow!'

I waved back. 'Okay.'

Except... was I going to see her tomorrow? I tiny knot inside made me feel bad for the little girl because, if I had my way, I was never coming back here again.

The car backed up then drove out into the tiny lane. I watched it go then turned back towards the stable yard. With its muck and its smells and its horrible girls.

I stood still for a moment, unwilling to take a first step back towards the yard.

Oh my god – I was so hungry.

'They seem to like you.' I turned and saw the round lady looking over her garden fence at me. Had Allie called her Jane? I assumed she was talking about Kate and her mum.

'They're nice.'

'Yes, they are. And how's your first day going?'

'Okay.' But I couldn't make the word sound convincing.

Jane nodded, with an I-understand look. 'Some of the girls can be a bit difficult.'

Difficult? If she meant bitchy, then I agreed. But I just shrugged.

'Your mum popped back and left this,' she held up a lunchbox.

Oh no... what was mum thinking? It was one of Freya's lunchboxes, the old one with Charlie Bear on the front. Even Freya had decided she was too old for it.

I glanced towards the stable yard. I really didn't want to take a little kid's lunchbox down there. Not that I wanted to eat with any of those girls anyway.

Jane must've read the look on my face, because she said, 'I've got a table in my garden, you can use that if you want.'

Jane sat with me and chatted while I ate. I asked her questions about the stables, until I started to feel stupid about how little I knew. But she was nice, and she didn't treat me like an idiot. After I'd finished, she said she'd look after my lunchbox and told me to go and find Allie to ask for more jobs to do.

I slouched out of her garden, dawdled down through the carpark, and then traipsed into the stable yard. The absolute last person in the world I wanted to find was Allie. She was bound to give me the worst job she could think of.

I glanced down at my clothes. At least I couldn't get much dirtier.

There was no one in sight in the yard. I walked down to the gap that led to the menage and glanced along there. Someone was riding around in the big space on a clumpy off-white horse. Maybe everyone was in the office watching them. Boring!

I looked around the yard again. Still no one. My eyes came to rest on the livery stables down at the end. The bottom doors were shut now... hadn't me and Kate left them open? Maybe the horses were back inside now.

I walked down towards them, bee-lining for the one at the far right.

I'd asked Jane what 'liveries' meant when I was in her garden, and she'd told me they were horses where their owners paid for them to be fed and looked after, so that all they had to do was come down and ride them.

That sounded like rich people. So, did that mean their horses would be really special?

I tip-toed the last few metres to the far-right stable and peered inside.

A golden pony looked up from a hanging bag of dried grass. She had liquid brown eyes and a thick white mane and tail.

'Oh my god, you're beautiful.'

Those eyes locked with mine for a few moments, then she tossed her head and went back to eating. It made me smile. I'd been dismissed.

'Oi! New girl!' Shouted from behind me.

Oh no! That sounded like Allie.

I turned away from the stable and saw her stalking down the yard. She had a fork clenched in both hands like she was going to attack me with it. Instead, when she reached me, she just shoved into my hands. 'Take this and tidy up the muck heap!'

What? I'd spent my whole morning going up to the muck heap... it didn't seem the sort of thing that could ever be made 'tidy'.

'How?'

'How?' She made her goofy face at me again. 'Are you stupid or something? Go up and take a look. It's a mess, and I'm telling you to tidy it up!'

There was no point in arguing. I'd expected to get an awful job, and this sounded like the worst.

She wasn't going to move out of the way, so I had to walk round her before I could head back up the yard.

As I went, I heard someone giggling. Probably Allie's friends watching from around a corner somewhere. No way I was giving them the satisfaction of looking round. I strode quickly past all the stables and up into the carpark, where the muck heap was fenced off in a small space on its own.

I stopped short when I saw it.

This morning when I'd dumped my last wheelbarrow of dirty straw it had looked messy for sure.

But now?

Someone... probably more than one someone... had been up here raking it apart. The concrete floor of the space was now strewn knee-deep with brown-smeared straw.

Allie and her friends? Probably. They must've had a right laugh.

I could've gone and told Jane. Or rung up mum to ask her to come and get me. Or gone and found Allie and had it out with her.

But what I actually did was start forking the straw and muck back into a pile. Something had changed. God knows why... but I suddenly didn't want to leave the stables anymore.

Was it because I'd be letting down little Kate? Maybe.

Or because of that pony, with her liquid brown eyes and that imperious look she'd given me, and the fact that some part of me wanted to see her again? Possibly.

Or... was it really because of what Allie and her friends had just done... and if I went crying to Jane or mum now, or if I left and never came back again, then they'd just think they'd won? Definitely.

I dug into the straw and kept heaving as fast as I could. The sooner I got this done, the less fun it would be for those idiots.

By the time I finished sweat was trickling down the middle of my back and my arms were falling out of their sockets.

I stood back and leaned on the fork. Good enough.

Then Jane's voice came from behind me. 'What are you doing up here?'

I turned and smiled. 'Just tidying up, I'm done now.'

'Great! You look like you need a break.' She beamed. 'I'm doing a lesson... why not come down and make a tea and watch?'

I did make a tea. Not because I liked it, but because Allie and her gang were lounging in the office, and it meant I could go in there and face them and make out I didn't care about their stupid trick.

'You finished the muck heap?' Allie asked as I went in.

'Yeah, no problem.'

I clicked on the kettle and it started boiling almost straight away.

'Hope it didn't ruin your Uggs,' one of the others said to my back as I poured hot water into a cup and dropped in a tea bag.

'These?' I glanced down at my feet. 'They're just old things.'

I added a dribble of milk and dropped the tea bag into a bin on the floor.

'Expensive, though,' a further voice tried.

I turned and gave them all an innocent smile. 'Not to me.'

I took my tea and walked back out of the office. I wanted to watch the lesson, but no way I was doing it in there with that lot. I walked back along the narrow path outside and stopped at the gate into the menage.

Jane was standing out in the middle watching a girl ride around on a reddy-brown pony. It looked bigger than that beautiful pony down in the livery stables, but not as big as the white clumpy horse I'd glimpsed in here earlier.

'Heels down, back straight!' Jane called out.

The girl on the pony was pretty with blond hair peeping out from under a rounded black helmet. She was staring straight ahead, her face rigid with concentration.

'Now trot!'

The girl kicked with her heels and started bobbing up and down. As she came past the gate, I saw she was moving in time with the pony.

'And canter!'

Canter? That's what Kate had been talking about this morning.

The girl kicked again and the pony seemed to fall forwards into a faster, rolling kind of run. The girl stopped bobbing and started moving backwards and forwards.

I forgot my tea as I watched the girl go round the menage, going back to a trot then into a canter again, even 'changing legs' when she cantered diagonally across the menage to change direction and go round it the other way. I didn't know what 'changing legs' was, but the pony seemed to do a little skip when it did it.

Finally Jane got her to practice trotting over some red and white polls laid on the ground down the centre of the menage and then jump over a small jump. The pony seemed to really love that, and the girl had to hold it back to stop it going too fast.

'Okay Chloe, that's it for today. Well done!'

And the girl dropped the pony back to a walk and took a relaxed couple of laps around the edges of the menage.

Jane came over and shoed me away from the gate so she could open it. 'What did you think of that?' She asked me.

'Amazing.'

She beamed, then turned round to call to the girl on the pony.

'That's enough cooling down, Chloe, bring her out now and give her a brush.'

And then Jane was walking away.

Part of me wanted to run after her. Ask if there was any chance I could try riding sometime. But she was sure to just laugh at me. What idiot comes to work at a stable when they'd never even sat on a horse?

The girl had climbed down off her pony and was leading it out through the gate.

'That was really cool,' I said to her as she went by.

She looked up and smiled. 'Thanks, I'm just learning though.'

'Well, it looked amazing.'

'Thanks, I'm Chloe by the way.'

'Poppy.'

Then a loud voice barked from right behind me. 'Chloe!'

Allie had come out of the office with her friends.

Chloe glared Allie's way. 'I'll talk to who I want, Allie.' Then she flashed me another smile and led her pony away over the cracked concrete of the yard.

What Chloe had said made me think... had Allie told everyone here not to talk to me?

Then I was slammed into the fence as Allie pushed past behind me. Then each of her friends did the same. I put up with two of them, but when the last one went past I'd had enough. I shoved her so hard she clattered against the side of the office. She was smaller than the others, with brown hair and clutching a small rucksack to her chest. She gave me a shocked look and muttered 'sorry' then hurried away.

Dah-dah, da-de-da-de-da.

My phone's stupid Star Wars alert tone went off and made me jump. I fished it out of my 501's pocket and clicked it to shut it up. It was dad's old phone and I really needed to find time to change everything on it.

There was a text from mum on the home screen.

I'm in the car park

She was here already? I swiped the screen to check the time.

17.22

How had it got that late?

I headed up to the car park and saw mum waiting by the car. 'So how was your day?' She asked.

29

Good question.

There'd been good parts; Jane and how she was so friendly, Chloe and the amazing way she rode, little Kate and that naughty Bella, and... I went warm inside... that beautiful golden pony down in the liveries.

And bad parts; mainly just Allie and her stupid friends.

But no way I was letting them get to me.

'Well?' Prompted mum.

I smiled. 'Best day ever.'

3
Kate's Lesson

'Are you sure you're okay, coming back down here again today?'

What was with mum? One day it was all 'you can't hang around the house all summer' and 'it'll be a great way to make friends'... and the next she kept asking if I was okay.

I glanced sideways at her as we turned into the lane to the stables. 'Yes, I'm okay.'

'And are the other girls being nice?'

'Not really. But I don't care.'

Mum's grip was tense on the wheel as she tried to get up the lane without grounding the exhaust.

'Why don't you care?'

Parents! They wanted to know everything.

'Not of all of them are terrible... there's a girl called Chloe, she seems nice, and there's this really sweet little girl called Kate.'

Mum turned the car into the carpark and pulled in at the side. 'They sound nice.' She'd already zoned out again, thinking about work or something.

As I got out of the car she reached around and grabbed something from the back seat. 'Don't forget your lunch.'

Oh no. Charlie Bear again!

But I took it and pushed the door shut.

Mum whirred the passenger window open a gap and called out. 'Have a good day...'. And then she backed up and drove away.

I glanced around the car park. There was no-one in sight. I looked across towards Jane's bungalow. No-one there either.

Oh well – better go down to the yard and see what jobs I was being lumbered with today.

I dawdled down to the end of the car park. The puddles had shrunk after a full day of sun yesterday. I glanced up at the blue sky. It looked like it was going to be hot again today.

I still had my UGGs on. They were pretty much trashed despite mum's efforts to clean them last night, so I'd decided to keep on wearing them. The same applied to my 501's. Mum'd put them through the washing machine and got rid of most of the brown marks, but there was no way I was ever wearing them out in civilisation again.

When I got to the yard it was already busy.

'Hello,' little Kate ran up and hugged me. 'You came back.'

Her hug only reached to around my waist. I disentangled myself and bent down to her eye-level. 'I said I would.'

'Sometimes people don't.'

Then a voice shouted from the other end of the yard. 'Oi, new girl!'

No prizes for guessing who that was. Allie was waving her arms from the bottom of the yard.

I smiled at Kate. 'I think she wants me.'

I walked down, not hurrying on purpose.

'Finally!' She spat as I reached her. 'I've been here since eight.'

I shrugged, guessing it was about 9 o'clock now. 'This is when mum drops me off.'

We were down near the livery stables, and I peered over her shoulder to see into the one on the far right. The whole door was open and I saw it was empty, and something sank inside me.

'Whatever!' said Allie, and I saw her eyes drift downwards. 'That your lunchbox?'

'Yeah.'

I kept it close against my leg so she couldn't see the front.

'Stash it in the office... then I've got a special job for you.'

I expected the 'special job' to be more mucking out but Allie took me past the line of livery stables to a path that wound between some bushes to...

Wow! A massive open field with fences around it.

Someone had talked about the paddocks yesterday. This must be them.

I picked out details as we got nearer. There were more fences that subdivided the huge space. And there were wooden structures with open sides dotted around.

There was a wide, closed gate right at the front but we didn't go through it. Allie took us down another path that led along the outside fence of the paddocks.

Suddenly there was a thudding of hooves.

And the beautiful livery pony stopped up against the fence and poked her head over.

The sight of her lifted me inside. 'Hello!'

Allie snorted. 'Horses don't understand hello.'

But the pony tossed her head up and down like she did understand.

I walked up close and reached to stroke her nose like Kate had showed me with Bella yesterday. Her fur was super silky smooth, and her brown eyes looked deep into mine.

'What's her name?'

Allie made a dismissive noise and batted my hand away. 'What's it to you?'

The pony jumped backwards and made a long snickering sound. I watched her in alarm. 'Are you okay?'

She shook her head, her mane flying.

I'm fine... I don't care about her!

I smiled, 'Good for you.'

My name's Kyra.

'Kyra?'

Allie made her goofy face and splayed her hands. 'If you already knew her name, why'd you ask?'

And she walked off, continuing down the path we'd been following. 'Come on, stop wasting time.'

I turned back to the pony and found she was still staring at me. 'Did you just speak to me?' I whispered. 'Or am I going nuts?'

Kyra twisted away and sprang into a gallop towards the far end of the paddock.

At the end of the path was a huge wooden barn. It had walls on three sides and was wide open at the front. And inside there were piles of squared-off shapes made of dried grassy stuff.

Allie pointed to the right side. 'That side's the straw bales.'

I nodded. The yellow bales looked like clean versions of what I'd been mucking out yesterday.

'And the other side's the hay.'

The bales that side were more greenish and looked like what I'd seen the horses eating.

Allie pointed back to the right side again.

'All those straw bales need to be moved to the back and stacked up, so there's room for the next delivery'.

Loads of bales were scattered around the floor of the barn.

Allie was walking away again. 'And don't spend all day doing it!' She disappeared back the way we'd come.

I shook my head. This seemed like a made-up job to me. Those bales looked heavy... and surely if they really needed moving then everyone would come down and help.

Yet here I was, on my second day, doing it on my own.

But... Jane had told me to do whatever jobs Allie gave me to do.

I went over to the nearest bale and tried picking it up by the strings that held it together. I could just about get it off the ground.

But did I need to pick these things up? I grabbed hold of the strings again and tried dragging the bale instead. A lot easier.

Twenty bales later I was exhausted.

I slumped down on the bale I'd just finished moving and pulled my phone out of my back pocket.

11.30.

It felt later than that.

I put the phone away and gazed out of the barn. Directly in front was a wide gravelly space, and beyond that an open area of scrappy long grass, and finally there was a line of tall trees.

The gravelly space had to be where trucks came to deliver the hay and straw.

My eyes dropped back to the straw bales I still had to move. I was about halfway through. I was going to be wiped out by the time I finished.

37

Then my eyes flicked up at a movement...
someone had just walked around the corner of the
front of the barn.

I groaned... not Allie again?

But it was someone else. Tall and slim, with
blonde hair tied back.

She was looking around. 'Poppy!' She called out.

'Over here,' I called back and waved so she could
see me.

She came over and I saw it was Chloe, that girl
from the menage yesterday.

'Jane sent me to look for you. She wondered
where you were.'

'Didn't Allie tell her?'

She shrugged. 'No. She just said you were
skiving off somewhere.'

Nice! That proved Allie had made this job up.
And now she was trying to get me into trouble too.

'She brought me down here.'

Chloe sat down next to me on the bale. 'What
for?'

'To move these straw bales to the back.'

'Why? The delivery guys do that.'

Yeah. That made sense.

'I think Allie's just making up jobs for me.'

Chloe gave me a twisty smile. 'Must've been what they've been whispering about in the office.'

'Allie and the others?'

Chloe nodded.

I imagined them sitting there, Allie telling them what she'd got me doing, and all of them laughing and making 'duh' faces.

'Look, I'm sorry if they're your friends, Chloe, but they're a bunch of witches.'

Chloe snorted a short laugh. 'Witches! That fits. But don't worry, they're not my friends. They're horrible to everyone.'

'Why do you all put up with it?'

Chloe made a not-much-choice face. 'Allie's a right bully. You should see what she's like at school.'

School? I hadn't given much thought to school. But after the summer holidays I was going to have to start at a new one.

'What school d'you go to?'

'Fairholme High.'

That sounded familiar. Did that mean I was going to have to put up with Allie at school as well?

But... whatever... that was a long way off yet. For now the summer holidays seemed like they stretched out ahead forever.

Suddenly Chloe jumped up like she'd remembered something. 'Anyway... you need to come. Jane wants you to watch Kate's lesson.'

Me and Chloe just made it back up to the yard in time for the start of Kate's lesson.

Jane was out in the middle of the menage again, and little Kate was on top of Bella, walking her slowly around the edge.

Chloe seemed worried. 'Something always spooks Bella.'

I remembered what Kate had said to me yesterday. 'When she tries to canter?'

'Yes, how'd you know?'

'Kate said something about it yesterday.'

We were watching from the menage gate. I didn't want to hang out in the office, not with Allie and her friends in there, and it seemed Chloe felt the same.

Besides, it was a lovely hot day.

Jane called out. 'Now, trot!'

Kate kicked at the sides of the little fat horse, and it jumped forwards into a trot.

I smiled at Kate as she came round past the gate and she smiled back, although there was something in her face that looked like she was nearer to tears.

'I hope she'll be okay today,' Chloe muttered. 'It's so good for her to keep riding.'

She must mean Kate.

'Why's it good for her?'

'Well, she's, you know... special.'

And I thought about Kate and how she was yesterday, and how protective her mum had seemed. Kate was lovely, but I got what Chloe was saying.

Kate and Bella had trotted around the menage three times now.

I heard low laughter drift out of the office.

Jane called out again from the middle of the menage. 'Now, canter!'

I saw Kate's legs kick and Bella leapt forwards out of her trot, like I remembered Chloe's pony doing yesterday.

Kate settled into a rolling rhythm on top of little Bella.

'Yes,' Chloe breathed from next to me.

But then Bella lurched sideways away from the edge of the menage, at the same time as shrieks of delight burst out through the open door of the office.

Kate hung on for a few moments, but Bella was bucking and running out of control towards the menage gate, where me and Chloe were standing. I heard a short scream and saw Kate bounce off Bella's back and sprawl onto the ground.

'Get Bella!' I said as, without thinking, I climbed up and over the gate and ran to where Kate was sitting up and wailing on the sandy floor of the menage.

'Poppy...' The little girl sobbed as I knelt down and hugged her.

'Are you okay?' I whispered.

'Nooo...'

Stupid question. I tried again. 'Are you hurt?'

'I don't think so,' she managed.

I helped her back onto her feet. She was still sniffling but at least the wailing had stopped.

Hoofs plopped up next to us. 'I got her.' Chloe's voice.

I kept an arm hugging close around Kate's shoulders as we turned towards Chloe and Bella.

The little horse was tossing her head, pulling Chloe's arm backwards and forwards where she held onto some leather straps around her face.

This was the first time I'd seen a horse up close which was being ridden. I kind of knew people used reins to steer a horse, but now I saw they were connected up to a metal thing that stuck out each side of the horse's mouth. And that was all held in place by thin leather straps that went around the horse's nose and up over its head.

Bella wasn't looking super-cheeky like the last time I saw her. She looked like she'd seen a ghost. Her eyes were rolling showing white around their edges. And it felt like she would run away again if Chloe let go of her.

'What's scared you so much?' I wondered.

The little lights.

'What?' I whispered. Had Bella just spoken to me? Like Kyra had this morning when she told me her name. Was I going crazy, or what?

And then something went *pip* and I saw a spark out of the corner of my eye. I looked round to see what it was, but there was nothing there.

Meanwhile Bella had half reared and pulled back, and Chloe was having a hard time hanging onto her.

'Here, let me take her.' I reached and took a hold of the leather straps where Chloe was gripping them. Chloe let go and after a few moments Bella calmed down again.

I leaned my head close to hers. 'I don't know what that little light was, but it can't hurt you.'

Pip!

Another one sparked, this time behind Bella's head. I saw it clearly, just a tiny dot of light and then it was gone.

'See, it didn't hurt,' I whispered.

Bella's eyes stopped rolling.

Pip!

Another spark came off to my left, and this time Bella hardly jumped.

What were they? I'd heard of fireflies, but never seen one. Did they even exist in England?

Kate pressed into my side, and I realised she'd been listening to me the whole time. 'D'you think Bella understands?'

I'm scared.

'I think she's scared.'

'I'm scared too,' said Kate. 'I don't wanna fall off again.'

Then Jane was there next to us, squatting down to get Kate's attention. 'Do you think you can try again, Kate?'

Kate came back with a small voice. 'Don't know.'

Jane smiled kindly. 'Just for a little walk round?'

Kate glanced at me. 'Maybe if Poppy keeps hold of her.'

I found Jane looking at me and I nodded. 'Of course, and I won't let go, Kate.'

Kate was so brave getting back on that pony. I could tell she was sore from her fall by the little gasps she let out as she heaved herself up.

When Kate was settled Jane went back to the middle of the menage.

Chloe was already back at the gate and was watching from there, and I felt a sudden weight of responsibility. What if Bella spooked again and I couldn't hold her? What if Kate got hurt for real this time?

'All right... walk on!' Jane called out.

I bent down close to Bella's ear and whispered. 'Remember, they can't hurt you.'

You sure?

'Yeah. And don't run away again, or you might hurt Kate.'

45

And then Bella was walking and I was keeping pace. We made it halfway round the edge of the menage, then...

Pip! Pip! Pip!

Three sparks lit up all round Bella's head.

I let out a squeak and held on tight, but Bella just kept on walking.

You're right, they don't hurt.

Phew!

I kept going and grinned at Chloe as we went past the gate.

'Do you want to try a trot?' Jane called out.

'Okay,' Kate called back and kicked with her little riding boots.

I had to jog to keep up.

Pip!

A spark came right in my face this time. It made me flinch but had no effect on Bella.

'Let go, Poppy!' Came Kate's little voice, tight with determination.

Kate kicked again and Bella lunged forwards out of my grasp. I stopped and watched as Kate and Bella cantered away.

'Well done, Kate!' Shouted Jane.

Bella didn't spook again, and Kate was beaming when she finished her lesson.

Chloe and I held the gate to the menage open as she and Jane led Bella out.

'You did it!' Chloe exclaimed.

'I know,' said Kate.

I was about to say how clever she was when a new voice came from behind us.

'Oh, well done, Kate!' It was Kate's mum.

'Mum! Did you see?'

'I saw.'

'Bella was wonderful.'

'She was. And I think you deserve a treat. Are you ready to go now?'

Kate's face went unsure. 'I've got to untack Bella and stuff.'

Chloe cut in. 'I'll do that Kate, then you can go with your mum.'

'Okay, thanks.' Kate let Chloe take hold of Bella.

'Yes, thanks.' Kate's mum said and then they were walking away, Kate chattering away and telling her mum about her lesson.

Chloe started to lead Bella away.

'Do you need any help?' I asked.

'No...' Chloe glanced back and shook her head. 'There's really only room for one person at a time in Bella's stable.'

As I watched them go I wondered what those sparks had been that had spooked Bella.

I would've asked Jane if she'd seen them, but she was already halfway up the stable yard heading for her bungalow.

The laughing that had been coming out of the office earlier had gone quiet.

Were those girls still in there? Was all this something to do with them?

I pushed the menage gate shut and started along the path that led to the door of the office. I wanted to see what they were doing... and I needed to get my lunchbox anyway.

I opened the door and they all looked up. Allie and her two biggest friends squashed on the sofa, and the small, quiet one perched on a rickety chair tight up against the far wall.

'Oh look, here's the big hero,' Allie mumbled. She had a carrier bag laid out on her lap and was talking through a mouthful of sandwich.

The girls next to her let out snidely little giggles, while the one on the chair just stared at the floor.

'Was it you lot that spooked Bella?'

Allie gave a pretend-outraged look. 'We were in here the whole time.'

But the two next to her kept giggling, like it was all some big joke that a pony had run away with a little girl and could've really hurt her.

I went to ask them about the sparky things, but then I stopped... they'd just be all 'what are you going on about' and 'you're such a weirdo'... or whatever. It wasn't worth it.

I bent down under the bench to where the lunchboxes and bags were stashed and looked for Charlie Bear.

'Really love the lunchbox, by the way,' Allie sneered.

I found it and pulled it out.

'Yeah, really grown up.' One of the others chimed in.

I stood up, ready to leave. But... Charlie Bear felt lighter than this morning. I unzipped the box and, even before I looked inside, I knew something was wrong.

Charlie bear was empty.

'Oh dear, did someone eat your lunch?'

I glared at Allie. 'Did you do this?'

'What if I did?' Allie stood up, her carrier bag falling off her lap and sending crumbs across the floor. 'Wanna make something of it?

She was a head taller than me, and there was a lot of her. I remembered what Chloe had said about her being a bully at school.

'Can't be bothered,' I turned away and escaped through the office door, slamming it behind me. Their shrieks of laughter echoed in my head all the way up the yard.

I wasn't sure where I was going with my empty lunchbox, but I ended up stumbling to a halt in the car park next to Jane's bungalow.

I should've stayed and stood up to Allie.

But I'd just run away.

'Are you okay?' Jane was in her garden right near the fence, kneeling down and looking up at me. It looked like she was digging a hole for a plant or something.

I wasn't going to tell tales.

'I forgot to pack my sandwiches.'

Jane gave my lunchbox an odd look. Then her face twisted into something disapproving. I was pretty sure she'd guessed what had happened to my sandwiches.

'Well. Food I can help you with. Come inside.'

I had no choice but to open the gate into Jane's garden, then follow her as she led the way to the back door of her tatty bungalow.

The inside of it was a shock.

It was nice.

Or at least, the kitchen was. It was huge with a big cooker and an island and wood cupboards. It was like on one of those makeover programmes on TV, after they'd done all the work.

Jane perched me on a stool at a breakfast bar at the far end of the island.

'Is ham okay?'

'Yeah, ham's great.'

She cut slices from a big loaf of bread then went over to a fridge and grabbed stuff out of it.

'Butter?'

'Yeah.'

And half a minute later I had a huge ham sandwich in front of me, along with a glass of water.

I took a bite into it. It was delicious.

Jane must've seen the look on my face because she said. 'Glad you like it.'

Then she was bustling towards the door to go outside again. 'Take your time, I need to talk to Allie.'

Rather you than me, I thought as she went out and shut the door after her.

And then I was on my own.

Thank god!

Out in the yard it felt like there was always someone watching. Laughing when I did something dumb. Even laughing when I didn't do something dumb.

But in here it was quiet, and calm, and not-so-awful.

The sandwich really was amazing. It was just ham, and bread, and butter. But the ham was cut thick, not like out of a supermarket packet. And I'd never tasted bread this fresh. And the butter... well, butter's just butter. But all of it together made every bite completely yummy.

I looked around the kitchen as I ate.

The cooker had those big heavy covers you have to lift up to cook stuff, and there was a nameplate with AGA printed on it at the front. The worksurfaces were light wood, and all of the cupboard doors. The fridge was a big double-doored thing with an ice maker on the front.

Everything was clean and tidy and nice.

Not what I'd expected.

As I started on the second half of my sandwich, I found myself gazing at a shelf up at eye-level next to the cooker. It was jammed full of recipe books.

Jamie's Christmas. Persiana. British classics. Simple.

Loads of them. All vaguely familiar from mum's books at home.

But then... blocked together at the right-hand end.

Eye of newt. Slugs and snails. Moon magicce. Herbal lore. Sugar and Spice. Everyday booke of spells.

What? A quarter of the shelf was filled with books with weird titles.

I only had one bite of my sandwich left, so I stuffed it into my mouth and jumped down off the stool.

53

Up closer it was clear the weird books were old. Their spines were creased like ancient bibles and, when I reached out to touch one, it felt warm, more like soft leather than the paper spines of the cookery books.

Something made me check the door. It was still shut.

What if Jane came back?

My fingers made a space between two books and eased one down off the shelf.

Sugar and Spice.

A smell of old paper wafted up as I opened the book.

The pages felt thin but tough. And the words were in beautiful old-fashioned handwriting, except it was so neat I wondered if it was printed. I leafed through and saw drawings amongst the words... of bits of plants... pots and fires... strange pieces of apparatus.

I flicked back to the start again, and on the inside front page it read...

Hexes for Hellacious Young Ladies.

The door opened and Jane came back into the kitchen.

Busted!

I slammed the book shut.

Would she yell at me? Would she ring my mum and complain? Would she throw me out of the stables, there and then?

But she just went over and got my empty plate and glass and took them to a dishwasher at the far end of the kitchen.

'I see you found my books of spells,' she said in a mysterious-spooky voice.

'Uh... yeah.'

She came over and took the book out of my hands.

'Bit of a hobby. Quite fun, aren't they? You can get loads in second hand bookshops,' she returned the book to its space on the shelf. 'It's a shame magic's not real, I think the world might be better if it was.'

When I went back down to the yard the first person I saw was Allie, leaning against the wall between two stables, like she was waiting for me. 'Oi, you. Come over here.'

I took my time. I'd already decided, if she threatened me again, I wasn't going to back down. Even if it meant getting beaten up or something.

55

She gave me the evils the whole way until I stopped in front of her.

'What did you tell Jane?'

I shrugged. 'Nothing.'

She glared for a few more moments.

'Lucky for you.'

Then she turned away and headed towards the gap that led to the menage and the office. As she went, she shouted back over her shoulder. 'Do what you like this afternoon, I don't care.'

Had Jane told her off? Back when she'd left me alone in the kitchen... she'd said something about finding Allie and talking to her.

But... did it really matter?

I was free, for the afternoon at least. I looked around. What should I do?

A lot of the stables had both doors wide open, so their horses must be out in the paddocks. But some just had their top doors open. Up near the top a big black head was looking out.

I walked over and the horse watched me all the way. A nameplate on the stable door said *SADE*.

Duh! Had there been a nameplate on Kyra's stable too? Was that how I knew her name? What an idiot I was, thinking she'd spoken to me!

'Hello Sade,' I wasn't sure how to pronounce her name.

Its Shar-day.

I stopped short and stared at the horse. 'Did you just speak?'

I felt like an idiot all over again. Horses don't speak. Sade hadn't moved her lips or anything.

The horse snorted and shook her head. But she didn't say anything else.

I stroked her nose. I had to reach up to do it, she was enormous.

'I wonder who you belong to?'

Jane.

Jane? It made sense that she'd have such a beautiful horse.

Wait!

'Did you just speak again?'

Sade just backed away into her stable and started chomping clumps of hay from a net hanging inside.

I watched her for a few moments. What was it with these talking horses?

'Hi Poppy!'

I turned and saw Chloe walking towards me.

'Hi Chloe.'

'Where've you been?'

I nodded up towards where Jane's bungalow was hidden behind the bushes and trees around the carpark. 'Jane made me a sandwich.'

'What happened to your lunch?'

I made a face. 'Allie.'

'Oh, sorry.'

'Don't be.'

'No, I should've told you. I never leave my stuff in the office.'

'Don't worry, Jane was nice.'

Chloe's face lit up. 'Oh my god, did you see inside Jane's house?'

She seemed to think that was a big deal.

'Hasn't everyone been in there?'

'No... no one... come on, you've got to tell me all about it!'

Chloe grabbed my arm and walked me down the stable yard. 'Let's go down to the paddocks, where there's no one to listen in.'

4
Riding Kyra

As we walked down to the paddocks, I told Chloe about Allie being hacked off with me. 'She said to just do what I want this afternoon.'

'She's awful,' Chloe stated. 'But... at least that means we can hang out... I've got nothing I *absolutely* have to do until I get Eddie in tonight.'

'Is Eddie your pony?'

'Yeah.'

I thought about that for a second. 'Nice name.'

She laughed. 'He was called that when we got him.'

'Is that him over there?'

A pony at the far end of the first paddock looked like the one she'd been riding yesterday.

'Yeah. D'you want to go say hello?'

'Try and stop me.'

We opened the gate in the fence that led into the paddock. The mud near the gate was churned up and not quite dried out yet. I tried to hop over the worst bits and made Chloe laugh.

'You've got to get some proper boots.'

I glanced down at hers. They were black and close fitting and reached up to just below her knees, some kind of black rubber that looked easy to clean off.

'I guess I should.'

Eddie saw Chloe coming and started trotting towards us, but then he stopped halfway and I realised there was another fence between us and the far side of the paddock.

He was nodding his head over the fence in excitement as we reached him.

'Eddie, this is my new friend Poppy,' Chloe said to him.

He made a noise something like a horsey laugh.

Chloe laughed. 'He whinnied! That means he likes you.'

'Hello Eddie.'

Hello.

Not again!

I didn't react. I didn't want Chloe to think I was nuts.

Chloe turned to me as she stroked Eddie's nose. 'So, what was it like – inside Jane's house?'

I made a surprised face and shrugged. 'Nice.'

'Nice?'

'Yeah. She's got this lovely kitchen with a big island with a breakfast bar and really nice cabinets and everything!'

'No!'

'And she's got one of those big cookers with covers on the top... and she's got a massive fridge with an ice maker.'

'And was the sandwich she made you all manky?'

'No. That was nice too.'

Chloe shook her head. 'I thought it would be all grotty and weird in there.'

'No, it was lovely,' I started, but then remembered the books. 'Although there was something a bit weird.'

'What?'

I hesitated. Jane had said her books were just a hobby... but I wasn't sure I quite believed it. Would she want me telling people about them?

'I'm not sure I should say...'

Chloe jumped on that. 'Not sure? You can't just dangle something like that and not tell me!'

'Well... d'you promise not to tell anyone else?'

'Of course... now spill.'

'She had these books on the shelf near the cooker.'

'What, like recipe books?'

'She had some of those,' I dropped my voice to a whisper. 'But then she had some others, that looked really old, and had strange names.'

'Like what?'

'Like... eye of newt... and sugar and spice.'

'What?'

'I took one down and looked inside... and they were, like, books of magic spells.'

Chloe squealed with laughter. 'Jane doesn't look like the witchy type!'

I laughed too. 'No, she doesn't.'

But inside I thought that maybe she kind of did.

After the paddocks we went down to the barn and hung out there sitting on bales of straw.

Chloe told me all about her school, where I was going once the summer holidays were over. It sounded big, and not too bad.

'So, it's okay then?'

'Mostly... except for the cool-girls brigade, you know, all plucked eyebrows and gonna-be-head-girl-one-day attitude, you know?'

I nodded. I did know, I used to be one of them back where I used to live. But that all seemed stupid now.

'And, of course, there's Allie and her friends, who are a pain to everyone.'

'Are they the same lot that hang out with her here?'

'Pretty much, except there's more of them at school.'

Then Chloe asked me about where I'd moved from, and I told her about my old school, and my friends, and our old house.

'So you moved here without any warning?'

I shrugged. 'Yeah, something to do with dad's job.'

'Parents just don't get it, do they?'

'Tell me about it.'

Then Chloe's phone chimed. She got it out and swiped it and the chime stopped.

'Time to get Eddie in.'

We walked back up to the paddocks and Eddie was there at the fence again.

'He wants his feed,' Chloe laughed.

Chloe opened another gate into Eddie's section of the paddock and he trotted through and nuzzled her. She hitched a rope onto his head collar and we led him across the front part of the paddock towards the stables.

Suddenly hooves thudded on the grassy ground.

It was Kyra! I hadn't noticed her out here.

Chloe moved protectively in front of Eddie and the golden pony stopped short of us and reared up, pawing the air with her front hooves.

Chloe backed away. 'Careful of her, Poppy. She can be a bit funny.'

Then a voice called out.

'Kyra!'

It was Jane standing at the main gate into the paddock.

Kyra turned and galloped away, and by the time we reached the gate Jane was leading her away towards the stables.

Chloe turned to me and said in a low voice. 'She's going to lunge her. You should go and watch.'

'What's lunging?'

'You'll see. Go to the menage, I'll catch up when I've sorted Eddie.'

When we got back into the stables Chloe headed up towards the top of the yard but she shooed me off towards the menage.

When I got there, Jane was standing just inside with Kyra. She saw me coming and smiled. 'Oh Poppy, can you hold Kyra for me?'

The gate was open so I walked through and grabbed a rope that was looped loosely around Kyra's neck.

Jane picked up a tangle of leather straps that was hanging on the fence.

'What's that?' I asked.

'Her bridle. I like to lunge her with a bit in her mouth, to keep her used to it.'

I could've asked what lunging was, and what a bit was, and how it went in her mouth... but there was so much I didn't know I just kept quiet.

Jane did something with her hand that made Kyra open her mouth, and then eased a metal jointed bar in with her other hand.

Strange, putting a chunk of metal in a horse's mouth, but it didn't seem to bother Kyra. She just chomped on it while Jane pulled the rest of the bridle up over her head.

The bridle had reins which she handed to me while she took the rope off from round Kyra's neck.

Kyra nudged me with her head then shuffled on her hooves. She seemed excited.

'Steady...' Murmured Jane as she hauled up a saddle that had also been perched on the fence and settled it on Kyra's back. Then she buckled up a strap under her tummy and pulled it tight.

I couldn't help a question bubbling out.

'Are you going to ride her?'

'No... no one's riding her at the moment.' Jane said as she grabbed one final thing from the fence; it looked like another bridle but made of canvas. She put it over Kyra's head and fastened it on. Then she attached one end of a long rope to a metal catch on the front of it.

'Here, hold this.' She gave me the coils of rope in exchange for the leather reins.

The rope was flat and wide and seemed very light.

'One last thing...' Jane breathed and threw the reins over Kyra's neck, then twisted them together underneath and threaded another strap through them. '...that's to stop them coming forward when she goes into a canter.'

Canter?

But how would Kyra canter, with no one riding her?

Jane must've seen my questioning look because she grinned as she took the coiled rope back from me. 'You'll see.'

Jane led Kyra out into the middle of the menage.

'Well shut the gate then, stupid!'

Oh god. Allie had crept up behind me. I glanced round and saw her leaning on the menage fence. Her friends filed out of the office door behind her and leaned on the fence as well, except for the smallest, who hung back by the door.

Well, I wasn't going to run away. I stepped outside the menage and pulled the gate shut behind me. Then I turned and leaned on the gate.

Allie was only a couple of steps away. I heard her whisper something and I glanced round. And that set off a chorus of snorty laughs.

'Okay Kyra, walk on!' Jane's shout from the menage pulled my attention back to her.

She was slowly letting out that coiled rope so that Kyra walked around her in larger and larger circles. In her other hand she held a long whip thing which she held ready in the air just behind Kyra.

Jane let the rope out to its full length until Kyra was obediently walking round her in a big circle.

'Now, trot on!'

Jane waved the long whip at the same time as calling out, and Kyra jumped forwards into a trot.

She got the pony to drop back to a walk, and then trot again, at least five times, before she called out... 'Now, canter!'

Kyra leapt out of a trot into a canter.

It was like she was dancing. She was so neat and precise. And it seemed like her hooves hardly touched the ground at all.

'You're so beautiful,' I breathed. And regretted it instantly. There was another whisper next to me and another chorus of laughs.

'And trot!' Out in the school Kyra dropped back down into a graceful trot.

I gave Allie a long glare, and she glared back. 'Bet you couldn't ride her,' she hissed.

She was right, I'd never even sat on a horse, and there was no point pretending any different. 'No, I couldn't.'

Her friends did their normal snorty laughs.

'Bet you're too scared to, like, even sit on her,' Allie sneered.

'I've never sat on a horse.'

'What, never?' Allie spat scornfully.

'Yeah, never.'

She rolled her eyes and glanced around her friends. 'What an idiot!'

And they all laughed again.

I should've just left it. What did it matter what they thought? But instead, I found myself saying, in a loud voice to get their attention...

'But I'm not scared. And riding horses can't be that hard, can it?'

Allie glared back at me. 'Oh yeah, why not?'

''Cos you can do it.'

The laughing stopped like someone turned off a tap.

'What?' Allie spat out like a threat.

I opened my mouth to say something like... 'You heard.' But then Jane's voice cut in from right next to me. She was back at the gate now with Kyra next to her.

'Allie!'

Allie gave a big sigh. 'Yes, Jane.'

Jane paused and I thought for a moment she was going to tell her off, but then she just said, 'Will you look after Kyra and put her away.'

69

'No problem.'

Jane opened the menage gate and threw the coiled-up rope to Allie.

I had a slight sinking feeling. Why hadn't Jane hadn't asked me to do that? But I knew the answer really. I wouldn't have had a clue what to do.

Jane walked off and then I was stuck with Allie and her mates again.

'So... riding's easy, is it?' Allie snarled at me.

I shrugged. 'I could learn.'

'No time like the present.'

'What d'you mean?'

'Well, if you've got the guts to do it...' her friends were hanging around behind her, waiting to see what Allie was going to say next. '...and it's so easy. Why don't you hop up on Kyra and walk her round the menage?'

'Jane said no one was riding her at the moment.'

'Rubbish... we've all ridden her, haven't we?'

There was a bunch of sniggers and yeah-we-have's and it's-easy's. Although the smaller girl near the back muttered... 'not me.'

Allie sneered. 'Unless you're too scared.'

I glanced at Kyra. She seemed to be listening intently.

70

'I'm not scared.'

'Right then!'

Allie took off Kyra's canvas headcollar. Then she untwisted the reins and went to the saddle and pulled down metal foot-shaped things from both sides.

'There you go… you just need to put your feet in the stirrups and grab hold of the reins, and you're off.'

Oh my god! What had I got myself into? I had no idea what to do, and I had a feeling Jane would be really angry if she found out.

'I'll help you up…' Allie was waiting next to Kyra.

I couldn't back out now.

I got a hold on the top of the saddle and Allie grabbed my knee and shin and boosted me up.

God! It was strange. With Kyra's gorgeous mane and her head in front of me, and me being so far up off the ground.

'Get the reins, then,' Allie snarled.

I vaguely remembered how I'd seen Chloe and Kate holding their reins, and I tried to do the same. Then I also remembered the stirrups, and waved my feet around until I got them into them.

'Now, go!'

I heard a slapping sound behind me, and Kyra skittered sideways and forwards. Had Allie just hit Kyra to get her moving? By the jeers coming from her friends, I decided she had.

But Kyra steadied and then went back to walking.

'I don't know what I'm doing,' I whispered.

But I do.

Hearing Kyra, however it was I was hearing her, made me feel better. Maybe this would work out okay.

I got all the way to the back of the menage before it all went wrong.

'WHAT THE HELL ARE YOU DOING!'

There was a tremendous shout from the gate, and I looked around to see Jane standing there waving her arms.

'GET DOWN FROM THERE THIS MINUTE!'

Oh god, she sounded cross. I needed to get off. But before I could do anything Kyra went crazy.

It was like she dropped away beneath me and I was in free-fall for an instant. Then the saddle slammed back up and threw me sideways. I got the sense of frantic hooves scrabbling underneath me, and then we were accelerating back towards the gate of the menage.

I caught a frozen image of everyone standing there; Jane still waving frantically, Allie sneering and laughing with her friends, and Chloe frozen on the path leading to the menage with her mouth open in a shocked O.

Then Kyra dived sideways again and was spinning round and round and the saddle kept hitting me hard and launching me into the air. But somehow it always caught me again. And whenever I slipped sideways and thought I was going to fall, Kyra seemed to dive underneath me and scoop me up.

The stirrups were clanking and hitting me on the ankles and the reins were snaking and whiplashing as I tried to hang onto them. And we were spinning so fast everything around me was a blur.

Then Kyra lunged forwards and hurtled away to the back of the menage again, before swerving along the back fence, and galloping back down the other side. I just clung on tight with my legs and clutched the front of the saddle.

We flashed past the gate and it seemed like everyone had gone quiet. Even Allie and her friends had stopped laughing.

Kyra did two more circuits of the menage, before suddenly digging in her hooves at the very back and sliding to a halt. I would've flown over her head for sure, except she kind of leaned backwards at the last minute so I slammed into her neck.

Then we were standing still next to the back fence as if nothing had happened. I pushed myself back into the saddle again. What had that been all about?

I like you.

Oh my god! Was Kyra speaking to me again?

'I like you too, Kyra...' I leaned forwards and hugged around her neck. 'But, can we not do that again?'

The pony snickered like she was laughing. Then she turned and trotted back to the menage gate, with me jouncing around on her saddle and feeling more likely to fall off than when she'd been hurtling around.

Kyra stopped at the gate.

Jane didn't say anything, she just stared up at me with a strange look of her face.

Suddenly I remembered, she'd yelled at me to get off Kyra.

How did I do that? I tried heaving one leg up and over Kyra's back so I ended up laying on my tummy on the saddle. What next? I let myself drop.

It was further down than I thought.

My legs gave way when I hit the ground and I fell over.

5

Facing The Music

My bedroom ceiling slowly got lighter as the sun came up outside.

Except it wasn't really my ceiling, not the one I'd grown up with. It was the ceiling in a tiny bedroom in a rented house. Mum and dad had told me and Freya they were looking for a new house and promised we'd get lovely big bedrooms, but for now I felt crammed in... uncomfortable... and out of place.

And on top of that I felt terrible about what had happened at the stables yesterday.

I should never have let Allie get to me. I should've been, like, 'Yeah, I am scared, so would you be if you'd never ridden a horse', and then walked away.

But I hadn't. I'd been stupid. I'd done exactly what she wanted me to do.

She'd known what Kyra was like, known she'd freak out if anyone tried to ride her.

She and her friends must've been hoping I'd get thrown off and hurt.

But we'd shown them... me and Kyra.

It was all kind of jumbled in my head, all the bucking and spinning and hurtling around, but I had some really clear flashes of being sure I was going to fall, and Kyra somehow scooping me up every time.

She hadn't been trying to throw me off or hurt me. But she'd freaked out for some reason... God knows what.

What she'd said, or what I thought she'd said, played back in my head.

I like you.

Something twisted inside my tummy.

What if I never got to ride her again? What if I never got to even see her again?

Jane had been so cross last night; suppose she didn't even want me back at the stables? After I'd collapsed in a heap, she hadn't tried to help me up. She'd just grabbed Kyra's reins and walked away.

'Go and wait in the carpark,' she'd called back over her shoulder. 'Your mum'll be here soon.'

The drive to the stables that morning whizzed by too fast. I didn't want to get there. I was convinced that Jane would be waiting in the car park to tell me to go back home.

We bounced and jolted into the car park, and I scanned the stony, rutted space. No one was waiting – in fact no one was in sight at all.

'Don't forget your lunchbox,' mum said.

I'd been too ashamed to tell mum about what'd happened yesterday, so she didn't know why I was looking around as she was trying to hand me Charlie Bear.

'Is there something wrong?' She asked.

'What? No.' I took Charlie Bear from her.

'I've got to get back for a TEAMS call.'

I unclicked my seatbelt, opened the car door, and stepped out.

The puddles were all gone now, dried out by the hot sunny days. The ground was even starting to look dusty.

'See you later,' mum called as I pushed the door shut.

And then she was backing out and driving away.

I looked around... still no one.

Then suddenly there was a creak and a squeak and a wheelbarrow appeared from up the path from the stables.

Allie's face lit up as she saw me. The opposite of what usually happened. Not a good sign.

'Jane's in the office,' she said as she clanked towards the muck heap. 'She wants to see you.'

Oh no!

But... there was no point in putting it off. If I hung around here Allie would finish emptying her wheelbarrow then have a great time escorting me down to the office like a prison guard.

I hurried towards the stable yard.

When I got there it all seemed so normal. Girls were rushing around getting things done. Someone I didn't know was leading a horse towards the paddocks.

'Hi Poppy!' And little Kate was suddenly there. 'Jane wants to see you.'

I gave her a weak smile. 'I know... thank you.'

'Are you in trouble?'

'Hope not.'

I trudged between the rows of stables and through the gap to the menage and then met Chloe coming the other way. Her face twisted into something between a smile and a wince of pity, it would've made a great emoji. 'She's waiting for you...'

'I know.'

She squeezed my arm. 'She just asked me a load of stuff about you... and I told her you're great.'

'Thanks.'

And then I was on the little path between the menage fence and the side of the office. Ahead of me the office door was open.

I peeped in. 'Hello.'

Jane looked up from behind her desk. 'There you are, Poppy. Come in and shut the door.' She wasn't smiling.

She waved me to a chair in front of the desk.

'I'm really sorry!' I blurted as I sat down. Suddenly my nose itched, and my eyes watered.

Her face remained a stony mask. I was so used to her being smiley that it was scary.

'Please let me stay.' Tears brimmed out of my eyes and started dribbling down my cheeks. 'Please.'

The stony look disappeared and became one of surprise. 'Let you stay?'

'Yes, I should never have got on Kyra, I know that. It was stupid and dangerous... I only did it because...'

And then I stumbled to a halt. I couldn't blame Allie. She'd set me up. But I'd been the one who'd decided to climb onto Kyra. I suddenly realised that, somewhere deep inside, I'd wanted to ride her... and that was why I'd taken Allie's dare.

'Because what?'

'Because...' I took a deep breath in. 'I wanted more than anything in the world to ride her.'

Jane finally smiled.

'Well done,' she said. 'Well done. It would've been easy to blame someone else. In fact, I'd already decided someone else was to blame. But what you just said has helped me make up my mind.'

'About what?'

Jane paused. 'I'll tell you later... when I've thought it through properly.'

I didn't know what to say. Was she making up her mind about letting me stay? Or was she talking about something else?

'In the meantime,' she went on. 'You need to learn that, in future, you should ask permission before you ride someone else's horse.'

I nodded. 'I have learned. I really have.'

'Maybe... but to help you remember... I've got a job for you today. Everyone's least favourite job.'

What, worse than all the jobs Allie got me to do?

'Okay.'

What else could I say?

Jane gave me the job of cleaning out the feed store.

She took me down to the livery stables and along a path that went past the right-hand side of them. As we went by Kyra's stable I glanced in, but she wasn't there.

'Here,' Jane said as she reached the end of the path and pointed at a shed connected to the back of the stable block. 'This is the feed store.'

She opened the door and inside the whole floor was crowded with black bins with lids, and semi-transparent tubs, and half opened sacks – all scrawled with people's or horse's names in marker pen. There were also all sorts of containers stacked on shelves around the sides and the back.

'Everyone in this place is sloppy,' Jane shook her head. 'And so the floor gets to be a mess.'

She pulled on a cord hanging down inside and a light came on.

She was right. Brownish pellets and half rotten carrots and something that looked like oats and other gunky stuff were all strewn between the bins and containers.

'And the problem is, apart from basic hygiene, it encourages rats.'

Rats!

I scanned around the floor again. I'd never seen a rat. Well, maybe I'd seen one on TV, or in a zoo. But not a real one, not in the flesh, well, in the fur.

I thought that maybe I might not like them much.

There was no sign of anything moving at the moment. But then, if I was a rat, I'd probably be hiding.

'All you need to do is get all of these bins and stuff out, then give the floor a good sweep out and a wash, then put it all back in again.'

I nodded. 'Okay...' I wasn't actually sure I could get it all done on my own.

'Good. And while you're doing it, really think about whether you've learned about asking before you do things.'

'I will.'

Jane walked away, then called back over her shoulder like she does. 'And you need to finish before evening feed-time.'

If I was going to get this done, I needed to start straight away. I went into the store and tried to pick up a black round bin near the door. No way I could get it off the floor. But by leaning it over a bit I could roll it along on its bottom edge.

I'd got it halfway to the door when I stopped.

How was I going to remember where everything went back? It might look a mess, but everyone was bound to know where their stuff was. And they wouldn't thank me for jumbling it all up.

My phone!

I pulled it out of my back pocket and long-pressed the camera icon on the home screen.

Right!

I took a picture from the doorway first. Then I went back in and took more pictures of each part of the store. Finally I took a video, scanning slowly around all the bins and sacks. That had to be enough, surely, to make sure I could get everything back in the right place.

As I was videoing, I heard a scrabbling sound. Rats? Yuck! This was going to be a horrible job.

For the next three hours I heaved and slid and dragged everything out of the shed and onto the path outside.

Finally the shed was empty. I checked the time my phone.

14.27.

Normally I'd have had lunch by now. But there was no way I was going to get finished if I stopped.

Then suddenly there was a, 'Hi Poppy,' from behind me.

It was Chloe.

'Jane told me to bring these.' She had a roll of bin-liners and a broom in one hand, and a plastic container in the other. 'The bags are for the rubbish... and this stuff is disinfectant for the floor.'

'Thanks.'

She dumped them next to the door. 'Sorry I can't stay and help... Jane said I couldn't.'

I smiled. She was so nice.

'Don't worry.'

She gave a little wave and then she was gone again.

I grabbed the broom and went back inside to look around the floor.

The whole while I'd been moving stuff I'd heard scuffles and scampering noises from amongst the bins. And I'd been ready for something furry and ratty to appear, scurrying around the bottom of the bins or running for the door. But there'd been nothing. And now the whole of the floor was clear, there was still nothing.

So much for there being rats in here!

I started sweeping up the pellets and the oats and the carrots and gunky stuff, getting it into small piles then holding the edge of a binbag flat between my feet and brushing each pile in.

Finally, I got it clean enough to just brush the final little bits out of the door.

Right... I looked around... the floor was solid concrete and I'd got the whole lot clean, even in the corners. I'd actually managed to fill two bin bags up to halfway.

And now all I had to do was to brush some disinfectant around, let it dry for a bit, then put everything back in.

But first... I really needed the loo.

I left the bags and the brush and all the bins and hurried away along the path, then past the liveries, and up through the stable yard to a small building just off the carpark.

Thank god! No-one was in there. I was desperate.

On the way back I realised I was really thirsty, and I stopped by Chloe's stable. She wasn't in there, but that was where we hid our lunchboxes now. I grabbed my water bottle and headed back down the yard.

Just as I got to the path to the feed store I met Allie coming the other way.

She gave me a sickly smile. 'Looks like you're doing a great job.' And she walked off.

What was she doing down there?

No!

I ran down the path. All the bins were where I left them on the path, but... the two bags were gone.

I went into the feed store.

'That bitch!' I growled, almost shocking myself.

The bags were by the wall. And they were empty. And all the mess was strewn back over the floor.

I stalked out of the feed store and along the path into the yard. I didn't know what I was going to do, but I couldn't just let Allie get away with this.

I headed for the office. She was bound to be in there, laughing and being horrible with the rest of her gang. I stamped along the path to the office then slammed open the door.

'Hello Poppy!'

Little Kate beamed up at me from a chair in front of Jane's desk. Beyond her I registered Kate's mum in another chair, turning and smiling my way as well. Finally, I saw Jane behind her desk, head on one side in a silent question.

'I'm so sorry,' I blurted. 'I was looking for Allie.'

Jane didn't smile. 'She just left for the day, Poppy... dentist I think.'

'Sorry...' I muttered again and backed out quickly.

Oh my god! Could I screw up any more today?

I stomped back to the feed store. How was I going to get it finished now, with all that mess back on the floor?

I reached the end of the path and stopped in mid-stride.

What?

Where were all the bins... and all the sacks... and everything else?

The only things on the path outside the feed store door were the two bin bags, the ones I'd been using earlier, but they were both half full again, as though Allie had never come down here and emptied them out.

The door to the feed store was closed up tight. I pressed down its catch and eased it open. Then I groped for the cord that switched on the light and pulled it down.

No!

All the bins and everything were back in place, like they had been before I'd started working here this morning. I peered down at the floor between the bins. It looked clean! And was it a little damp too? I bent down and touched it with my fingers, then brought them up to my nose to sniff. Definitely a faint smell of disinfectant.

I glanced around, looking for the disinfectant container. And there it was, just inside the door. But half empty, although I'd swear it had been full when Chloe brought it earlier.

Chloe?

Had she come and done this for me? But how could she, though? I'd only been gone a few minutes. Maybe she'd brought everyone from the stables to help. But even then, was it possible? I shook my head... that must've been what happened. What other explanation could there be?

I picked up the disinfectant, shut the door, and went to go and find Chloe to thank her.

She was nowhere in the yard, and I already knew she wasn't in the office or near the menage. That left just the paddocks or the hay barn.

I bumped into her as I soon as I started down the path to the paddocks. She was heaving a wheelbarrow with a whole bale of straw balanced across it back towards the stables.

'Sorry, I can't stop or I'll never get started again,' she panted.

'I'll help.'

I jumped in next to her and grabbed one of the wheelbarrow's handles with both hands.

'Thanks,' she gasped, moving so she had the other handle with both hands too.

Between us it was much easier to push wheelbarrow with its bale of straw along the path and into the stable yard.

'The least I could do, after the amazing help you gave me.'

'What?'

'You know, after Allie threw all that gunk back out onto the floor of the feed store.'

'She did what?'

'Emptied my bin bags of gunk back out... when I was in the loo.'

'How horrible!'

This conversation was starting to get weird. We reached the yard and finally dropped the wheelbarrow down onto its runners.

'But you already knew that, didn't you?'

Chloe shook her head. 'How would I?'

'So...' I glanced towards the path to the feed store. 'You didn't clear it all up for me, and disinfect the floor, and then put all the bins back in?'

Even as I said the words, they sounded completely ridiculous. How could anyone have got that all that done in the time I'd been away searching for Allie?

'No.'

I let out a long breath of confusion. 'Then, who did?' I whispered, half to myself.

'Poppy!' Jane's voice made me look up.

She was walking up the yard with Kate and her mum.

I managed a smile, despite the confusion clattering around in my head.

'Have you finished the feed store?'

'Yes... I think I have.'

'Good... because Kate and her mum would like a word with you.'

Everyone was smiling, so it couldn't be anything bad. But I had no idea why they'd want to talk to me.

'Walk with us back to the carpark,' Jane suggested, heading off without waiting for anyone to say yes or no.

Chloe was already cutting strings around the straw bale and breaking out chunks. 'Catch up with you later,' she whispered.

I nodded and followed Jane, Kate and her mum.

We all headed for Kate's mum's car and stopped next to it.

Kate's mum fixed me with a steady gaze. 'Kate didn't have such a good lesson today.'

'Oh no, what happened?'

'I didn't fall off...' Objected Kate.

Kate's mum glanced down. 'No, you didn't, you were very clever,' then she looked at me again. 'But Bella ran off with her again.'

I remembered those weird sparks in the air yesterday, and the *pip* noises. Had they set Bella off again? I wondered if Allie and her friends had been having another good laugh.

But... I couldn't go round making accusations if I wasn't sure.

I bent down and looked into Kate's face. Her eyes were puffy and red from crying. 'Are you okay now?'

The little girl nodded. 'I think so.'

'She had such a good time yesterday,' Kate's mum said.

I stood up again and nodded. 'Yeah... She walked and trotted, and even told me to let go of Bella so she could canter.'

'But that was when you were in there with her.' Kate's mum's eyes searched mine, like she was looking for something. 'She really likes you... and yesterday, somehow, you made everything work out all right.'

I wasn't sure what I'd done, really. Other than talk to Bella and tell her not to be frightened. Unless I'd imagined all that. I certainly wasn't going to tell Kate's mum or Jane about it.

'I've had a chat with Jane,' Kate's mum went on, and the two grown-ups shared a short glance. 'We wondered if you'd be willing to help Kate on a more formal basis.'

'What d'you mean?'

'Maybe you could spend time working with Kate every day... and in particular, be in the menage with her when she has her lessons?'

'Please!' Kate squealed up at me.

I glanced down into her excited face. 'Yeah, I'd love to.'

I'd have done it anyway, I liked Kate... but this also sounded like a great way to get out of being bossed around by Allie.

Mum arrived early at the stables to pick me up that day. She'd warned me with a text message that said something about needing to get home for another TEAMS call.

I should've told Jane I was going early, but I kept avoiding it. What she'd said that morning about thinking something over and talking to me later kept running through my mind. It couldn't be anything like chucking me out of the stables, not now I'd agreed to work with Kate, but it must be something important. I was dreading it being something to do with Kyra, like banning me from ever going near her again. If it was that, then I didn't want to know.

Jane spotted me from her garden as I hurried across the carpark. She got up from whatever she was doing and waved. 'Poppy, can we have that chat?'

'Sorry, mum's early. She's in a hurry.'

Did Jane look cross? Hard to tell from this distance. But she waved both hands in an it-doesn't-matter kind of way and sounded okay when she called back. 'That's fine. We'll talk tomorrow.'

That night I sat on our sofa in the squashed lounge of our rented house. I was on my own; dad wasn't home yet, mum was still on her call, and Freya was already in bed. My old friends had been on Snapchat all evening, and I'd been watching the banter go backwards and forwards and chipping in sometimes. Even though they'd all asked about me, I was feeling more and more left out. New things were happening in their lives that I just didn't know anything about.

I finally got fed up and dropped off the chat and ended up staring at the wall.

I could watch TV... or flick through some TikToks... or find a youtube. But I didn't feel like doing any of that stuff.

I couldn't get my mind off everything that was happening at the stables; the chat Jane wanted to have with me tomorrow, me starting to work with Kate and Bella, and how I was going to deal Allie and her awful friends. And then there was all the weird stuff that was going on there; talking horses, the weird sparky things in air in the menage, and that job in the feed store getting finished all on its own.

The feed store... there was just no way one person, or even loads of people, could've got all that muck back off the floor in the time I'd been away, let alone scrub it down with disinfectant and put all the bins back in! I remembered the pictures and the video I'd taken... just getting all the bins and stuff back in the right places would've taken ages.

I picked up my phone and went to the photo app. The pictures of the bins were still there. I sighed, no point in keeping them now. I started clicking through them. Quick look, delete. Quick look, delete. Quick look, delete. Quick look... wait... what was that?

It looked like a face, down between two of the bins. Or was it just a weird pattern on the floor?

I used two fingers to zoom in... until...

Oh my god!

It was a little face. Peeking out between the bins. And it had a little body underneath, and a kind of bent-over pointy hat on its head.

It looked kind of like a garden gnome. Except it didn't have a beard, or a fishing rod... and it looked more like a girl than a crinkly old man.

But I'd emptied out everything out of the store, and I didn't remember seeing anything like that.

I swiped to the next picture, and the phone made a crackling noise and the picture started moving – it was that video I took.

I watched as it ran through. Just bins, set out in jumbled rows, marker-penned like I remembered... but then, a flash of movement.

I pressed pause. Could I make it run slower? I tried pressing 'Edit' down at the bottom of the screen. It brought up a timeline strip under the video. I slid my finger along it... Yes! The video moved forwards a frame at a time.

I slid my finger the other way, taking it back to where I'd seen the flash of movement.

There...

God! The face was there again, with its little body and its hat.

I moved the video forwards... then backwards again... and kept doing it until I was sure that I was really seeing what I thought I was seeing.

It wasn't possible... but it was some kind of little person. Coming out from behind the bins and then jumping back again.

I got a sudden shiver and threw the phone across the sofa.

6
A Day of Surprises

I thought I'd never get to sleep that night.

Two questions kept cycling around in my head. What was Jane going to talk to me about in the morning? And, what the hell had that thing been in the feed store?

Whenever I managed to stop thinking about one, the other came back and tag-teamed me.

When my phone alarm went off I jerked so hard my arm knocked it off my bedside cabinet. I had to grope around on the floor to find it and kill the alarm.

'Are you up yet!' Mum called from downstairs.

Was it morning already? I felt awful.

'Nearly!' I yelled back.

I dragged myself out to the bathroom and showered and brushed my teeth, then got dressed and stumped downstairs.

Mum appeared when I was halfway through my cornflakes. 'Leaving in ten!' Then she was gone again.

Ten minutes... then a twenty-minute drive to the stables... then I'd have to face Jane.

When we arrived at the stables Jane was waiting in the car park. No chance for me to slip off down into the yard and put off our 'chat' any longer.

As mum drove away, she walked over. 'Come inside, I'll make you some tea.'

I had no choice but to follow her.

Her lovely kitchen was just as clean and tidy as it had been last time. Jane sat me at the breakfast bar again as she boiled a kettle. My gaze wandered to her shelf of books, and the weird leather-bound ones stacked at the right-hand side.

Were they really books of spells?

So much had been happening I hadn't really thought much more about them. But... books of magic spells kind of matched up with the other weird stuff going on at these stables.

Should I mention it all to Jane?

But what she said next, after she came and put my tea in front of me, made everything else fly right out of my head.

'Well Poppy... Great job by the way, on the feed store, I don't think it's ever been that clean.'

'Thanks.'

'But what I wanted to chat to you about was Kyra.'

'I've learned my lesson...' I blurted. 'I won't try to ride her again.'

Jane paused and considered what I'd said.

'I don't think I can accept that,' she said finally.

Oh no! Was she going to ban me from even seeing Kyra?

'The look on your face!' She laughed. 'Sorry, I shouldn't tease you.'

'What do you mean?'

'Well,' and she turned serious again. 'You need to know that Kyra hasn't been ridden for... well... a very long time.'

'Okay,' I had no idea where this was going.

'Her owner... went away. I miss her terribly. And Kyra... well, they had a very strong bond.'

'Is that why you lunge her?'

Jane nodded. 'It's the only way to keep her exercised. And I do it with her saddle and bridle on in the hope that, one day, she'll choose another rider.'

No wonder she'd got so cross when she'd seen me on Kyra.

'Which I never really thought would happen,' Jane went on. 'Until yesterday.'

What? What did she mean?

Jane leaned forwards. 'I think Kyra likes you.'

Was that a tear wobbling at the bottom of Jane's right eye?

I didn't trust myself to speak, so I just nodded. I knew Kyra liked me, because she'd already told me.

'So that's what I had to think through yesterday,' Jane went on. 'And I've made up my mind now.'

'About what?'

'Poppy, I'd like you to start looking after Kyra. You know, brushing her, doing her feeds, cleaning her stable, getting her in and out of the paddocks... everything.'

Was I still asleep at home? Was this a dream and my alarm was about to go off for real any moment?

'Well? Could you do that?' She prompted.

'Yes! Yes please! Thankyou. But...'

'But, what?'

'I don't know what I'm doing. I've never looked after a pony before.'

'Don't worry, I'll show you.'

My head was whirling. I imagined Kyra's pretty face, her deep brown eyes with their knowing look, her mane flying as she flicked her head.

'But you must make me a promise,' Jane's voice broke into my thoughts.

'What promise?'

'That you'll let me give you lessons on her as well. She's been too long without a rider.'

I left Jane's house in a daze. Had that just really happened? Was I really going to start looking after Kyra... and riding her too?

Back in Jane's kitchen, once I'd said yes, she'd gone through some details. She'd told me to focus on Kate today, sticking with her and helping look after Bella, and then being in her lesson. Then tomorrow, which was Saturday, we'd start with Kyra. Then, as I was heading out, she said one last thing... that because I was going to be so busy, I didn't have to do any jobs for Allie anymore.

The sun shone down on my face as I crossed the car park and headed down the path to the stable yard. Another lovely day. But it would've been lovely even if it had been pouring with rain!

I walked into the stable yard and smiled as I saw everyone bustling about. I searched around for Chloe, I was bursting to tell her my news.

But then I heard a sobbing, sniffling sound.

I stopped and glanced around. It seemed to be coming from the second stable down on the left-hand side.

Oh no! That was Bella's stable. Was that the sound of Kate crying?

The door was open, so I went over and stepped inside.

Bella was chewing through some hay while Kate was leaning with her head in her pony's mane again.

'What happened, Kate?'

'Oh Poppy!'

Kate turned and hugged me instead.

'What's wrong?'

'S'nuthing.'

'It must be something.'

'She said I'll never be a proper rider.'

'Who?'

'Gemma.'

I hadn't heard that name yet. I'd been so busy since I'd been here, I'd hardly met anyone properly. But I could take a guess at who she was.

'Is Gemma one of Allie's friends?'

I felt Kate's little head nod against my waist.

Then I heard someone whispering outside.

'Is she still in there?'

'Yeah, blubbing.'

'What a baby.'

'Suppose she tells Jane?'

'She's too scared.'

'We'd better make sure she is.'

It sounded like two girls. One had to be Gemma, and the other could be Allie, or one of her other friends.

Well, if I was going to help Kate, this would be a good time to start. I disentangled myself from the little girl. 'I'm just going outside for a bit.'

Kate's eyes went wide. 'But they're out there, I can hear them.'

I squeezed her shoulders. 'It'll be fine.'

I turned and walked back into the sunshine. Two girls were standing next to Bella's stable door. Neither of them was Allie, but I recognised them as two of her friends.

'Can I help you?'

Initial looks of shock on their faces turned into sneers.

'Oh, it's you,' one said, like I was something she just stepped in.

'What, not the little eight-year-old you were expecting?'

'What're you trying to say?' The other one snarled.

'That depends if you're Gemma.'

105

'What if I am?'

'Well, if you are, then I'm saying, you'd better leave Kate alone from now on.'

'Or what?'

'Or I'll get you thrown out of these stables.'

'You? You're just the new girl.'

'What if I told you Jane and Kate's mum asked me to look after Kate? What d'you think they'd do if I told them I caught you bullying her.'

'You wouldn't dare.' Gemma threatened, but her bottom lip quivered and gave her away.

'You'd be gone in a second.'

'I wouldn't,' Her face went red. 'But... just don't do it, right?' She spat.

'Leave her alone then.'

Gemma tried to give me a tough glare, but it wasn't working. Her friend pulled at her arm. 'Let's go, Gemma.'

'Just watch yourself.' Gemma muttered. 'You don't know what we can do.'

And then they were both hurrying away towards the path to the office. Probably to tell Allie all about it.

But since I wasn't her slave anymore, who cared?

I worked with Kate all morning, but I think I got more out of it than she did.

I got to see her routine for looking after Bella. And that had to be the same as I'd be doing with Kyra. The two ponies might look very different but underneath they were the same.

First we took Bella out to the paddocks. Kate explained that she normally put Bella in the closest segment of the first paddock, unless Cob or Blake were already in there, in which case she'd take Bella down the path to one of the other paddocks, because she never, ever put her with either of those horses. I asked if Cob and Blake were out here already, and she pointed out a clumpy, off-white horse in back segment of the first paddock. 'That's Cob, he belongs to Cindy. Cindy's nice, but Cob can be horrible.'

Cob was a long way off, mooching around near the fence by the trees at the very back. I thought he might be the horse I'd seen in the menage at the start of the week.

'Does anyone ever share a paddock with him?'

'Nuh-huh... no way!'

'And Blake?'

Kate peered around. 'He's not out yet.'

'So can we put Bella in the front segment here?'

Kate gave a big nod. 'Yes.'

There was already a horse eating grass out in the middle of the front segment, but Kate said her name was Sade and she was lovely.

Sade? Then I remembered, *Shar-day*.

'Jane's horse?'

Another big nod. 'Yes.'

We opened the gate and Kate un-hitched her rope from Bella's headcollar. The pony happily trotted off to stand near Sade, looking tiny against the huge black horse.

Next, we went back to the yard and mucked out Bella's stable. I'd already done plenty of mucking out but there was still one thing I didn't get. 'You know, after we pile the clean straw around the sides so the floor can dry...' I started. 'When does it get put back down on the floor again?'

'When the floor's dry, silly,' Kate said, peering up at me through those thick glasses. 'And then you have to get new straw to mix in with it and spread it out so it's comfy.'

I nodded. That made sense.

After that we did Bella's hay net. Kate unhooked it from just inside Bella's stable and we went to another storage shed that was down next to the feed store.

'This is where we get our hay and straw,' Kate told me.

Inside there were scattered bales of hay and straw, most of them broken apart.

'Don't you use the stuff from down in the barn?'

'Silly!' Kate giggled. 'It would take ages to keep going down there and back, that's why we bring some up here.'

'Who does that?' It sounded like a hard job, and I was a bit amazed I'd never been lumbered with it.

Kate shrugged. 'Not me, I'm too small.'

'Allie and Gemma?' I suggested.

Kate laughed and shook her head. 'They're too lazy.'

'Chloe, then,' I said, remembering helping with her wheelbarrow yesterday.

Another one of Kate's big nods. 'Yes, Chloe... mostly... sometimes other nice people.'

Kate refilled her net with hay she pulled out of a bale on the floor and heaved it towards me. 'Can you carry it?'

Then we backed out and closed the door again, but before taking it back to Bella's stable Kate stopped at the feed store and opened the door.

I backed away without realising what I was doing, and only stopped when sharp twigs poked me in the back. I looked round and found a thick bush behind me.

'I just need to get some other feed,' Kate said as she ducked inside, without even putting the light on.

I heard a hollow sound like the top of a plastic bin being taken off and put back on. And then Kate reappeared with a small paper sack with a picture of a pony on the front of it.

'It's a sulpa... supla...'

'Supplement?'

A big nod. 'Yes... that's what it is.'

I wasn't being clever, the bag had 'supplement' printed on it under the picture of the pony.

Kate latched the feed store door back shut and I let out a breath I hadn't realised I'd been holding. Had that little person-thing still been in there? Watching everything Kate did? Waiting to... I don't know... jump-scare her... or whatever.

Kate led the way back to Bella's stable and got me to hang the hay net inside. Then she poured some pellet-like things out of the paper sack into a rubbery plastic bowl down on the floor.

'And that's it!' She said, shooing me out of the stable and shutting the door.

A shout drifted down from the direction of the carpark. 'Half hour 'til your lesson, Kate!'

Jane was up there waving.

Kate suddenly looked panicky. 'I've got to get Bella!'

I put a hand on each of her shoulders. 'Don't worry, I'll help.'

Kate was hugging the paper sack still. 'But I need to take this back, too.'

I took the sack out of her arms and leaned against the wall outside Bella's stable. 'We'll do that later... now let's run down to the paddocks and get Bella quickly.'

Kate cheered up once she was running. She laughed as we skidded round past the livery stables and along the path to the paddocks. I let her beat me to the gate.

'I won!' She huffed.

'You did!'

'I never win.'

'I'll beat you next time,' and made a pretend-grrr type of face.

That made her laugh... until she looked into the paddock.

'Oh no, that's Blake!'

I looked up and saw Sade was no longer in the front part of the paddock with Bella. Instead a reddish-brown horse with a white stripe on its nose was in the middle of the paddock and starting to walk towards us, while Bella was cowering against the fence in the far corner.

'Blake kicked her last time,' Kate muttered.

'Why would anyone put him in here, then?'

'He's Allie's horse.'

Right! All morning either Allie or one of her friends had been hanging around watching us. Kate had filled me in on all their names; Allie and Gemma I already knew, but the others were Kim and Beverley. They seemed hacked off about something. Probably me threatening Gemma this morning. Or me not being their slave anymore.

But trying to take it out on Bella? That was a new level of nasty.

Blake reached the gate and stuck his nose over. I stroked him where his white stripe was... he seemed okay.

'You're not going to hurt Bella, are you?' I whispered.

Blake shook his head and snorted. Then his eyes rolled, and I saw whites round the edges.

'Oh no...' Kate whispered.

Blake backed up and cantered away, heading for Bella.

'Stop!' I shouted without thinking. It came out super loud and even shocked me.

Kate put he hands over her ears. 'Oww...'

And out in the paddock Blake dug in his front hooves and skidded to a halt.

I already had the gate open and was striding towards him. Something told me not to run... not to panic... just to be firm. Blake watched me coming. 'Don't you move, Blake!'

He didn't. I got a hold of his headcollar and then called back to Kate. 'I've got him, you get Bella.'

I heard Kate's rushing footsteps as she went past, then back again with her pony trotting after her. I didn't dare take my eyes off Blake.

He was big and heavy, and he stamped and shook his head a couple of times, trying to get away. He nearly pulled me off my feet, but I held on.

'Steady...' I breathed, copying what I'd heard Jane murmur to Kyra.

The paddock gate went thunk and I hoped that was Kate shutting it behind her.

Right... what now? Should I just let go of Blake's headcollar?

Something told me that was a bad idea.

Okay... the only other thing I could do was lead him back to the gate, like I would if I was taking him out. He followed me, still shaking and tossing his head, and when I got to the gate I opened it, slipped through, and closed it again, leaving him on the other side.

I held onto his head collar over the top of the gate a moment longer. 'Good boy...' I tried. But his eyes were rolling again.

I let him go and he reared up, pawing the air. I was glad the gate was between him and me. Then he turned and galloped away.

'Oh my god!' Chloe's voice came from behind me.

I turned round and saw her next to Kate and Bella, with another wheelbarrow-load of straw in front of her. She was shaking her head. 'That horse is off-the-scale crazy.'

'For sure,' I agreed.

'Poppy, you saved Bella...' Kate breathed quietly. The little girl was hugging her pony's neck and giving me a worshiping look.

I suddenly remembered her lesson.

'Come on, we've got to get Bella ready!'

As we rushed back up the path I called back to Chloe. 'See you later... I've got loads to tell you!'

We got Bella's saddle and bridle on as quick as we could. But even rushing I learned a lot about *tacking up* a pony; how tight to fasten the *girth* under their tummies, how to get them to open their mouth to get the metal *bit* in, and even the fact that everyone's saddles and bridles were kept in a *tack room* down at the bottom of the yard, attached to the end of the right-hand stable block.

Jane was waiting at the menage gate when we got there.

'Perfect!' She said, holding the gate open so we could walk in.

I was holding Bella's bridle again, like I had when I'd helped her in the menage before.

'Start walking her round!'

I led Bella along the front fence of the menage so that we went past the office. As I expected, Allie and her friends were in there. But I couldn't hear them laughing. Maybe Jane had spoken to them.

I continued up the long side of the menage away from the office, and then along the back fence and down the other side.

We walked around the menage twice while Jane stood in the middle and called out instructions. Like 'Sit tall, Kate,' and 'Gather up those reins,' and 'Keep your heels down.'

It sounded like a lot to remember, but I was looking forward to doing it myself when I started my own lessons on Kyra. The thought caught me by surprise and something inside soared.

'Now trot! And keep a hold of her Poppy.'

Kate kicked Bella's sides a couple of times and she broke into a trot. I had to jog along to keep up.

Every time we went past the office I listened out for shouting or giggling... but there was nothing!

And as we went around, I looked out for the sparky things in the air that went *Pip*... but didn't spot any.

'Bella...' I whispered between puffs. 'If you see any of those sparky things, remember they can't hurt you.'

Bella didn't reply this time, but her ears twitched and swivelled my way like she was listening.

'Let's try a canter! You may have to let go, Poppy.'

Kate kicked again and Bella leapt ahead. I kept up for about half the length of the menage then let go. Then I kept level with Bella by cutting in towards the middle of the menage and running in a smaller circle, all the time looking out for those sparky things.

But I didn't see anything, and Kate and Bella were great. Racing around the menage like they'd never had any problems at all.

'And... trot!'

Bella dropped down to a trot and I caught up with her and took the bridle again.

As we went past the menage gate I saw Chloe there, leaning against it.

'Well done, Kate!' She called out.

There was a small crowd of other girls with her, all of them smiling too.

We kept going for another half hour. Walking... trotting... cantering. Mostly around the sides of the menage, but sometimes cutting across on a diagonal so we could change direction and go around the menage the opposite way.

Finally, Jane came over as we were walking down the left-hand side.

'Well done, Kate!'

'Thankyou Jane.'

'And well done to you too, Poppy. Having you in here really seems to make a difference.'

I smiled. I wasn't so sure I'd made any difference. There'd been no sparks to spook Bella this time. And a suspicious quietness from the office each time we'd gone past it. But I had a tingly, icy feeling inside. With the way Allie and her friends had been staring at us all day, it felt like something could still happen.

I wasn't relaxing just yet.

'Just cool down with a couple of circuits walking, then put her away,' Jane said as she headed away towards the menage gate.

'There's mum!' Squealed Kate and waved frantically.

Kate's mum was now part of the crowd standing outside the menage gate. Jane said something to her and then they went away into the yard together.

The girls at the gate also started wandering off, and in moments there was only Chloe left there watching.

She smiled as we went past the gate. 'That was great, Kate.'

Then she saw my face and her smile dropped.

She mouthed words silently… 'What's wrong?'

I shrugged and kept leading Bella around the menage. Past the office again, then up the long side fence. Jane had said to take Bella round a couple of times, but I decided to cut that down to just once. In fact, why hadn't I just got Kate and Bella out of there when I'd just gone past the gate? Stupid, stupid, stupid.

Still, just one more circuit… we reached the back fence again and started along that… about another fifteen more paces and we'd turn back towards the gate again.

Then I felt a chill, like a cloud had covered up the sun, and a gust of wind swished the treetops and kicked up small dust tornadoes that skittered away across the dry surface of the menage.

'Oh no!' I heard Kate breathe.

I looked the same way she was staring, and… no way!

There was another horse in the menage, between us and the gate. Blake! With no saddle or bridle on, not even a head collar.

Beyond him Chloe was still leaning on the gate, like she couldn't even see him.

Blake reared up and waved his front hooves in the air, just like he had done in the paddock this morning, and then he charged towards us.

Bella squealed and twisted sideways, wrenching my arm. I held on tight to her bridle. If I let go, she was going to bolt.

Blake stopped short of us and twizzled around, like he was going to kick out. Bella danced backwards out of range, then turned around and tried to run.

'No Bella!' I yelled, and somehow held on, even though she dragged me for a dozen steps before I managed to stop her again.

Blake was going crazy. Jumping and bucking and spinning in circles. Was he going to run at us again?

Then a flash of movement caught my attention, right next to me on the ground under the side fence.

What?

A little face peered up at me. That thing from the feed store!

That horse isn't real.

Then Blake snorted and gathered himself to run at us again.

'It looks real,' I hissed.

The tiny person shook its head.

I can help if you ask me to.

'Yes!' I yelled. 'Please help!'

Blake wasn't stopping this time. He was going to charge right through us. And Bella was frantic, jumping and twisting and trying to get away from my hold on her bridle.

Phtzzzip!

A shower of sparks sprayed up into the air in front of Bella, Kate and me, and Blake ran straight into it.

And then... nothing.

Blake was gone. The sparks were gone. And when I looked back down at the fence, the little person was gone too.

Bella kept twisting and swizzling around for a few more seconds, so hard that she pulled me off my feet and I ended up dangling down still holding tight onto her bridle.

'Steady... steady...' I whispered.

She slowly calmed down and I pulled myself back onto my feet, keeping a tight hold on her bridle. Finally a had a chance to look at Kate to see if she was all right.

The little girl had her eyes screwed tight shut.

'It's okay, Kate. You're safe now.'

Kate opened her eyes and looked right at me. 'Is Blake gone?'

I nodded. 'He's gone... although I'm not sure he was ever really here.'

I kept hold of Bella until Kate got off, and then we led her out of the menage.

Chloe held the gate open as we went through, then followed us to Bella's stable.

'What was that all about?' She asked.

The way she said it made me sure she hadn't seen Blake in the menage. But I didn't want to get into that now, with Kate listening. 'I'll tell you later...'

'Okay, meet me in the barn when you're done,' she whispered. 'I'll get our lunchboxes.'

I helped Kate get Bella back to her stable and take off her saddle and bridle. The little girl was very quiet, but at least she wasn't crying. As we dropped Bella's stuff off in the tack room, I spotted someone waving from the end of the path that led to the car park.

'There's your mum.'

'Oh no.'

'Don't you want to see her?'

'Not like this.'

'Why not?'

'She's worrying a lot... she might stop me coming.'

'Would she do that?'

Kate gave a dunno-maybe kind of shrug.

I squatted down and looked into her eyes. 'Deep breath, Kate!'

She nodded and sucked one in.

'Now hold it!' I counted to five in my head. 'And let it go.'

Her lips got a bit less trembly.

'Now do it again.'

Three more breaths and she looked a lot better.

'You okay now?'

She nodded. 'I'm still scared, though.'

This wasn't right. This sort of thing shouldn't happen to a sweet little girl like Kate. 'I'll get it sorted.'

'Really?'

'Yes, really.' Although I didn't have a clue how.

'Okay.' And her face cleared and she smiled, and when she skipped up the yard towards her mum, it was like all her cares had disappeared.

I wished I could do that.

I found Chloe at the back of the barn sitting on a bale of straw.

'So, what made Bella flip out this time?' She asked as I sat down next to her.

'Didn't you see?'

Chloe shrugged. 'She just seemed to go crazy for no reason.'

I shook my head. 'There was a reason. There was another horse in the menage.'

'What?'

'Allie's horse, Blake... he was in there, running at us and trying to kick Bella.'

Chloe was shaking her head. 'There wasn't any other horse.'

I knew it! Chloe hadn't seen anything. Even though she'd been standing right at the menage gate.

'Maybe there wasn't...' I unzipped Charlie Bear and looked inside; I was suddenly starving. 'Maybe I'm just going nuts.'

Chloe was opening her lunchbox as well. 'Yuck... Egg mayo again.'

'At least I got tuna,' I said, chomping into a sandwich. 'And a KitKat.'

'Lucky you.'

'You can have half of the KitKat.'

'Thanks.'

My head was still reeling from what had happened in the menage, but there was a load of other stuff I wanted to tell Chloe.

'Did you hear I'm working with Kate now?'

Chloe nodded. 'I was there when Jane told Allie... she wasn't happy.'

'I bet... she's lost her slave.'

'But she'll get you back in the afternoons, won't she, after Kate's left?'

'No... 'cos Jane asked me to do something else as well.' A glow blossomed inside me that forced a smile to stretch my face. 'To start working with Kyra.'

'Kyra?'

I nodded.

'Oh my god... except for Allie, Jane never lets anyone near her.'

'Jane said Kyra likes me.'

'Wow!'

'And...' the glow reached my fingers and they tingled. 'She's going to give me lessons on her.'

Chloe went quiet for a heartbeat. 'But no one ever rides Kyra.'

'I know.'

'Is this for real?'

'Yeah.'

Chloe let out a brief laugh. 'Now that's really going to hack Allie off.'

'Why?'

'Before she got Blake, Allie desperately wanted to ride Kyra. She went on and on at Jane about it. Until Jane let her try once...'

My tummy went cold... Allie had ridden Kyra?

'... but Kyra threw her right off. Like, badly threw her off.'

The coldness seeped away. 'Good for Kyra.'

Chloe was zipping her lunchbox shut. 'You know,' she went on. 'If you're having lessons on Kyra, you might want to do them when Allie and her friends aren't around.'

'Why? I'm not scared of them.'

She gave me a disbelieving look. 'You should be. But that wasn't what I meant.'

'What did you mean then?'

'Okay... my turn to sound like I'm going nuts... but, that thing you said about Blake being in the menage, I don't not-believe you.'

'Does that mean you do believe me?'

She nodded. 'I haven't told anyone else, but something like that's happened to me too.'

'Really?'

'Yeah... a couple of weeks ago I was bringing straw up and my wheelbarrow tipped over in the yard... and Gemma was there and she laughed at me... and so I called her a lazy cow.'

'Sounds fair.'

'Anyway, she went all narky and stormed off, and I didn't think any more about it. Except then, the next day when I was practicing jumping, something sparked in front of Eddie's face and he dumped me into the middle of a jump.'

That sounded familiar. 'Did the spark make a *Pip* sound?'

Chloe stared. 'How'd you know?'

'That's happened to Kate and Bella too.'

Chloe shook her head and let out a long breath. 'It's got to be Allie and her friends who are doing all this.'

'Okay, but how?'

'No idea. But someone's going to get hurt if we don't find out and stop them.'

We both went quiet.

'I've got an idea,' Chloe said finally. 'They're always in the office when this stuff happens, right?'

I nodded.

'So, what if I go and sit in there with them next time Kate's in the menage. Then if they do something, I'll see what it is.'

Why hadn't I thought of that?

7
Allie's Accident

Chloe's plan had been a great one.

But as things turned out, we were going to have to wait before we could try it out.

The next day was Saturday, and when mum dropped me off in the carpark there was a big lorry parked in the middle with a ramp sloping out of the back.

As mum drove away, Allie came up from the yard leading Blake.

She gave me a sneery smile. 'Oh, hi Poppy. In case you're wondering, this is what you can do when you're a real rider.'

She led Blake towards the ramp. He started backing off as he got close, like he didn't want anything to do with getting inside a lorry, but Allie yelled at him and kept hauling on his lead rope until he gave in and skittered up the ramp.

I walked round and peered inside. Allie was busy tying up Blake and then swinging round a wooden gate-thing that bolted shut so he ended up standing sideways.

'Out of the way, new girl!'

I turned and there were Gemma and Kim, leading a dappled brown and white horse. It was smaller than Blake but heavier set with hairy feet, like a miniature carthorse. Gemma went up the ramp and it just plodded after her.

'God, are we bringing that thing?' Someone breathed from behind me.

I looked around and saw a middle-aged man. He gave me a distracted half-smile then yelled up into the lorry.

'Get them sorted girls, we don't want to be late!' He glanced up at the sky, which for the first time in days was overcast and grey. 'Hope it doesn't rain.'

Then he was gone, walking away towards the cab at the front of the lorry.

Where were they going?

I could've asked, but I'd only have got a sarky answer back, so I left them to it and headed down the path to the stable yard.

Halfway down someone else came rushing up the other way. Beverley, Allie's smallest friend. She was clutching her rucksack to her chest and peering at her phone, and I had to jump to the side so she didn't crash into me.

'Sorry!' She huffed, then ran past. I watched her go. She didn't seem so bad. She didn't radiate the same bad attitude as the rest of them.

I turned back towards the yard and found myself smiling.

Allie and her friends weren't going to be here today!

Jane was in the yard and called out the moment she saw me. 'Poppy! Let's make a start with Kyra.'

Jane must've seen me hesitate and glance at Bella's stable, because she added... 'Kate's okay to do Bella on her own this morning.'

That feeling of joy bloomed inside again. This was it!

The morning went by like a dream.

First Jane showed me how to put Kyra's headcollar on and we took her out to the paddocks. As I led her through the yard everyone turned and watched. There seemed to be a lot more people at the stables today. Some extra girls I'd not seen before and even a few adults too. Maybe because it was the weekend.

Jane told me she usually put Kyra in the front part of the second paddock. I asked if she ever shared with other horses, and Jane nodded. 'She's fine with any of them, she's quite able to look after herself.'

When we got there, I unhitched the rope from her collar and she bent her head and butted me gently until I stroked her nose, then she turned and galloped away across the grass.

I caught Jane smiling when I glanced around at her.

'I told you she liked you,' she said. 'Now, we can chat while you muck out.'

We went back to the yard and I grabbed a wheelbarrow and a fork and started on Kyra's stable.

Jane watched me work and starting running through everything I'd need to do to look after Kyra; how and when to groom her, what to feed her, how often her shoes got changed, when she got her teeth filed by the dentist, how to clean her saddle and bridle... on and on and on.

No way I was going to remember it all... it seemed like more than a full-time job. Not that I cared, I felt like I was in heaven.

Just before lunchtime I was back on Kate-duty.

I held onto Bella's bridle as Kate walked the little pony into the menage.

'Good luck, Kate!' I recognised Kate's mum's voice and smiled round at her. She wasn't usually here for Kate's lessons. She must not work on Saturdays.

As we walked along the fence at the front of the menage I saw Chloe heading into the office. She gave me a wave. Today she'd be able to sit and watch in luxury.

The lesson went great. As usual I held onto Bella when she walked and trotted, then let her go when she cantered.

When we came out Kate's mum looked like she was going to burst. 'Well done, Kate. And Bella, you were so good today.'

She gave my arm a brief squeeze and flashed me a thanks-so-much smile, before walking with Kate and Bella back to her stable.

'You seem to have solved Kate's problems with Bella,' Jane said from next to me as I watched them walk away.

It wasn't a question. Jane didn't seem to be asking what Kate's problems were, or how I'd solved them.

But should I tell her?

Yeah right! She was going to believe me about imaginary things appearing and spooking Bella, and how me and Chloe thought Allie was to blame. And while I was at it, I could tell her about the little person in the feed store, and the talking horses.

Then would she still think I was the right person to look after Kyra?

'Anyway,' she said, making me zone back in. 'Why don't you go and get Kyra? This seems like a good time to start teaching you to ride.'

The first thing Jane taught me was how to get up onto a pony properly.

'Hold the reins in your left hand and grab the front of the saddle.'

I did that.

'Don't let them hang like washing lines!'

I shortened the reins and tried again.

'Good... now left foot in the stirrup... right hand on the back of the saddle... and just jump up onto her.'

Easy.

Except when I saw her head and mane in front of me again I got a fluttery feeling inside. What if she ran off again?

I won't.

I hadn't even said anything out loud, but Kyra still knew what I was thinking.

The fluttery feeling started to fade away.

'Now, pull the right rein to turn her around... then a little kick to get her walking around the edge of the menage.'

Kyra hardly needed me to pull the rein... she turned on her own... and she started walking before I could give any sort of kick.

'This might actually be okay...' I heard Jane mutter.

Jane backed away towards the middle of the menage, watching us intently.

We reached the back corner and I gave a tiny tug on the left rein, and Kyra turned to walk along the back fence.

Oh my god. I was heading for the place where she'd freaked out before. The fluttery feeling came back inside me.

But Kyra just kept going, steadily walking to the next corner, then turning left again to follow the fence down the other side of the menage.

'Good... give her a nudge with your heels to speed up a little!'

I gave a small kick and the rhythm of her walk picked up.

'Shorten those reins!'

Jane kept calling out comments and directions as we walked two more circuits of the menage.

'Sit up straight!'

'Heels down!'

'You're going to have to get some proper boots!'

'Not so stiff... soften your arms to keep even pressure on the reins.'

'Relax those hips too, try to move with Kyra.'

'Good... good.'

She finally asked me to stop halfway along one side of the menage.

'Right. We're going to try a trot, and that'll be it for today.'

Trot? Just walking had been harder than I expected, what would trotting be like?

'You're going to want to rise up out of the saddle then back down again in rhythm with Kyra's trot.'

Okay... but what did that mean?

'So, try standing up now... while she's not moving.'

I tried.

'Not so high. And tilt more forward, or you'll get left behind. That's it... try to remember what that feels like.'

'Okay.'

'Now, sit down and up again, into the same position.'

Jane got me to do it a few more times, telling me when it looked right and when it looked wrong. It was hard enough to do with Kyra just standing there, what would it be like when she was moving?

'Right. Now let's try it for real.'

Jane got me walking again. The rest of the way up that side of the menage and then across the back. Then, when we were halfway back towards the front again, she said... 'You'll need to rise when her left shoulder goes forwards, Poppy. Now... Trot!'

I don't know if it was me kicking a little harder, or Kyra just heard what Jane wanted her to do, but she was suddenly going faster.

'Rise up and down, Poppy. Don't just bobble around.'

I tried doing it. Up when Kyra's left shoulder went forwards, down as it went back.

'That's it! Up... up... up...'

We reached the front of the menage and followed the fence around. I caught a glimpse of Chloe through the office windows, and she gave me a double thumbs-up.

Trotting felt weird at first, but after two circuits of the menage it began to feel a bit more natural.

Jane kept calling out the whole time.

'Sit up straight, don't hunch forwards.'

'Not just up and down... slightly forwards too, don't get left behind.'

'Don't stand on your toes... keep those heels down.'

It was a relief when she finally said... 'And... walk!'

But not for long. She made me trot again after another half-circuit of the menage. Then drop back to a walk. Then go forwards into a trot again.

I had knots of pain blossoming in weird places. In my thighs where I was sure I was holding on too hard. In my butt from slapping down on the saddle when I got the rhythm wrong. And on the inside of each calf where the stirrup straps kept pinching my skin.

'And... walk!' Jane said again, and she came over to walk beside Kyra.

Did that mean we'd finished? I hadn't expected to be relieved that my lesson on Kyra was over.

'How was that?' Jane asked.

I made a face. 'Hard.'

She grinned. 'It'll get easier, don't worry. You're a natural.'

A natural? I thought I'd been rubbish.

After the lesson Jane showed me how to untack Kyra, then put everything away, and then rub her down.

'Well done, Poppy!' Jane finally said as she left me outside Kyra's stable and headed back up the yard towards her house.

I was suddenly on my own, watching Kyra munching hay from her hay net. I still had lots of odd aches and pains from my lesson, but I couldn't wait to get back on her again. She had just been so wonderful.

'Poppy!'

I turned at the sound of feet running behind me. It was Chloe coming down the yard with her face all lit up.

'What?' I knew something must've happened.

'It's Allie!'

What had that girl done now? I already knew where she and her friends had been all day. Jane had told me while we'd been working with Kyra. Her dad had taken her to the Chelmsford county show so she could take part in an intermediary jumping competition. What if she'd managed to get a trophy and was now back to rub our faces in it?

'Did she win something?'

'No,' Chloe shook her head. 'That would be awful.'

'Then what?'

'She fell off.'

'No!'

'Yes... and she broke her leg.'

'No!'

I must be a terrible person, because a sudden laugh bubbled out of me before I could stop it.

Chloe clamped her hand over her mouth and giggled through her fingers. 'I did that too!'

The sound of hooves made us both look round. Gemma and Kim were leading Blake down the yard, their faces clenched in anger, while behind them Allie's other friend, Beverley, was leading the little dappled horse that'd gone with them. The smaller girl had her rucksack on her back and she didn't look angry, just pale and shaken.

Gemma and Kim opened Blake's stable and took him inside without a word.

'Where's Allie?' I whispered.

'A&E... her mum took her.'

Then I remembered the man from this morning. 'What about her dad?'

'He's just driven the horses back. I was up in the carpark when they arrived, that's how I know about Allie, I earwigged him telling Jane.'

Gemma and Kim came out of Blake's stable, slammed the bottom door shut, then stamped over to where Beverley was still holding the other horse by a stable on the other side of the yard.

'Is that Beverley's horse?' I asked Chloe.

'Yeah,' she whispered back. 'His name's Patch.'

Gemma hissed something at Beverley and shoved her in the shoulder. Beverley backed up against the stable wall and the two bigger girls crowded in close.

'I didn't!' I heard Beverley whine.

More hissed words and then Gemma pointed over at Blake's stable. Then the two bigger girls turned away and stalked up the yard. In moments they'd disappeared up the path that led to the carpark.

'What was all that about?'

Chloe shrugged. 'Dunno.'

Beverley stayed glued to the stable wall and stared after them like she expected them to come back. She looked petrified.

'Beverley isn't much like Allie and the others... why does she hang out with them?'

'Well...' Chloe started, and her tone told me this was going to be something juicy. 'She's not so much their friend, as their slave.'

'Slave? Like I was?'

Chloe shook her head. 'Way worse. She's their slave at school. She's a real sweat, top marks in everything, and that lot get her to do all their course work for them.'

'Why does she do it?'

'Because she's small and I 'spose she doesn't have anyone to stick up for her.'

'God! Why does she keep Patch at the same stables as Allie?'

Chloe shrugged. 'She had Patch here way before Allie started coming... I guess he's happy here, and she loves him more than she hates being bullied.'

I thought about Kyra. How long had I known her... a week? But I already totally understood how Beverley must feel.

Patch nuzzled Beverley and the girl seemed to snap out of her daze. She opened the stable door next to her and took the small pony in. She came straight back out with an empty hay net and rushed over to Blake's stable. She came out of there with another hay net and ran down the yard towards the hay store.

'Look's like she's got the job of looking after Blake.'

Chloe nodded. 'Yeah... I don't suppose we'll see Gemma or Kim down here again until Allie comes back.'

'You think?'

'I hope.'

And laughter erupted out of both of us that we didn't try to stop.

I was still at the stables after everyone had left that night. Mum had texted to say she and dad and Freya had gone to Lakeside shopping centre, and that they'd swing by to pick me up on the way back.

I didn't mind. The clouds had gone now and evening sun was slanting across the yard and I just waited by Kyra's stable while she hung her head over the top door and let me stroke her mane. It was so soft and silky. Jane said it had always been like that and hardly needed any combing to keep it nice.

My gaze wandered around the stable yard... then stopped at the sight of something outside Bella's stable.

Her paper sack of supplement pellets!

Was that still there from yesterday? Or had she just left it out again today?

Whichever... it should get put away. In case it rained or something.

But that would mean going to the feed store.

It wasn't like I hadn't been in there since I'd got those pictures of the little person. But it had always been during the day when there were loads of other people about. Did I really want to go in there now... when everything was all quiet and creepy?

My mind jumped back to when I'd seen it at the side of the menage, when it'd spoken to me.

I can help if you ask me to.

That's what it'd said.

At the time I'd been desperate. I hadn't hesitated to yell at it to help me. But now, thinking back... the way it'd spoken those words... deliberately, not rushed... was like an offer with strings attached.

I shook my head. Had I really seen it... and really heard it talking to me? It was all just too weird and wacky. Tiny people didn't exist, not in the real world.

I hadn't even told Chloe about it yet, even though we'd got into talking about sparks appearing in the air and phantom horses in the menage.

I sighed. None of this was getting Kate's sack put back into the feed store. Just the thought of it sent a chill jittering down the back of my neck all the way to my feet.

'Wish me luck,' I whispered to Kyra.

And I walked quickly over to Bella's stable and picked up the small paper sack. Then, before I could change my mind, I strode back down past Kyra's stable to the feed store.

Kyra snickered as I went by, like she was laughing at me.

Good luck.

Was that a horsey joke? If it was, I didn't appreciate it.

I lifted the catch on the feed store door and reached in to pull the string that put the light on.

The dim light seemed brighter than I remembered, and I realised that dusk was finally darkening the sky. I went in and found a black round bin with 'Bella' written on the side in white marker pen. I lifted the lid and put the sack inside.

I glanced around.

Nothing was jumping out and trying to scare me. And nothing was scuffling around making noises amongst the bins.

I could just run back out and slam the door.

No.

I walked to the door and pushed it shut. Then I went back to Bella's bin and leaned my butt on it.

'Okay... so, where are you?'

Absolute silence greeted my question.

'I know you're in here.'

More silence.

Then an owl hooted outside. And a distant car horn beeped from one of the roads beyond the end of the lane.

I took a big breath in, and a pet-shop smell of horse feed and oats and even a hint of garlic tickled at my nose.

'What do you want?' I tried.

A faint sound of a house door slamming shut drifted in from outside.

Otherwise, nothing.

Then...

Dah dah dah... dah de dah de dah.

I jumped so hard I slipped and fell sideways off the bin.

Bloody ring tone!

I staggered back onto my feet and pulled out my phone.

We are in carpark – sorry late xx

Mum!

I took a last look around the feed store. Everything was really still; the bins, the sacks, even the cobwebs hanging down from the roof.

I had to go. They were waiting for me.

I walked to the door, deliberately slowly. Did I feel like anything was watching me leave? Not really.

I pulled the door open, switched off the light and stepped back outside.

'There's a surprise at home!' Was the first thing Freya said as I got in the car.

'What is it, Mum?' I tried, and just got a 'wait and see' back.

'What is it, Dad?' But he just concentrated on driving, no way he was spilling if mum wasn't.

Whatever. We'd be home in less than twenty minutes anyway.

I changed the subject and asked what they'd bought. Lakeside was this huge shopping mall, just the other side of the Dartford Bridge. Back where we used to live I would've been super jealous about missing out on a shopping trip. Me and my friends used get dropped at the Trafford Centre and hang out there all day. But... I found I wasn't really bothered. Everything about my old life had started to seem unreal, like it had been someone else's.

'Just bits and pieces,' mum replied.

Ugh! It would've done my head in dragging around a load of shops getting *bits and pieces* all day.

I stopped talking and watched everything outside go by. This wasn't such a bad place to live. Kind of suburbia, but not run down or anything. Dad had told us it was commuter-distance to London, which made the houses more expensive and better looked after.

We turned into the estate where our rented house was. It was a mix of bungalows and houses with steep roofs and dormer windows. After a few left and right turns we pulled into our driveway.

'Looking forward to the surprise?' Freya giggled. She was very excited.

'Can't wait,' I said in an exaggerated-bored voice.

'Oh...' She said, disappointed. 'Here's a clue, her name's Seefa.'

'Freya!' Said mum, in a now-you-spoiled-it voice.

Her name? They hadn't gone and got a dog, had they? I hated dogs.

We got out of the car and mum and dad grabbed loads of carrier bags and hauled them to the front door. Then there was a lot of fuss opening the door and getting everything inside.

One good sign... I couldn't hear any barking or whining.

'There she is!' Freya squealed.

She grabbed up something from the ground. Something black and furry. She cuddled it to her then thrust it at me.

It was a cat... well, not much more than a kitten... black and fluffy and gorgeous. It purred and didn't struggle as I held it.

'Seefa was outside our back door this morning,' mum said. 'I checked with all the neighbours and went to the vet, but she's not chipped and no one knows who she belongs to.'

'So now she's ours!' Freya asserted.

Mum made a maybe sort of face. 'For now, anyway.'

Seefa's eyes were deep green and stared into mine like she knew me.

'Why Seefa?' I asked.

'Freya's idea. From the reading book I'm doing with her. *C for Cat*... so Seefa.'

'Get it?' Asked Freya.

I smiled. 'I get it.'

It was actually quite a cute name.

It wasn't long before Freya told me she hated me.

Seefa hung out with me the whole evening and completely ignored her; she sat on the floor gazing up at me during dinner, then she came and sat on my lap while we all watched *The Masked Singer*, and finally she came to my bedroom when I went up to Snapchat my old friends.

Seefa was a real hit on Snapchat. Everyone went on about her so much it made me feel properly part of my old group again.

She came with me when I went to the bathroom and waited while I brushed my teeth, then followed me back and jumped on my bed when I got in.

I gazed at her. 'Where did you come from?' I wondered.

I found myself holding my breath, half-expecting her to reply like the horses at the stables. But she just stared and blinked her eyes, then curled into a ball down near my feet.

'Goodnight Seefa,' I whispered, and switched out the light.

8

The Book of Spells

The next day dawned bright and sunny again. People on morning TV were starting to talk about water shortages and hosepipe bans, like they did whenever there were a few nice days in a row.

Last night Mum had gasped in disbelief when I'd asked for a lift to the stables again. 'Surely you're not going there on a Sunday!'

So I'd told her about my responsibilities; working with Kate and Bella, looking after Kyra, and helping Chloe getting hay and straw up from the barn.

And on top of that I needed to have my riding lesson.

Anyway, what would I do stuck at home all day?

A tiny meow had interrupted me at that point, and Seefa had jumped onto the back of the sofa and bumped my head with hers.

'Okay, I could play with you,' I'd said, stroking the cat between her ears. 'But Freya can do that too.'

Seefa had then jumped back onto the floor and stalked away, almost like she'd understood what I'd said.

And now she was watching me forlornly from halfway up the stairs as I headed for the open front door.

Mum called from outside. 'Come on, then… if you insist on going!' I heard her slam the car door.

I gave Seefa a final little wave and rushed out.

Sundays down at the stables turned out to be even more busy than Saturdays.

I asked Chloe about it when she came over to chat while I was doing Kyra's stable.

'Everyone comes down at weekends, especially Sundays,' she explained. 'All the usual people from the week, plus all the full liveries, and then there's everyone who comes for lessons.'

I'd seen Jane out in the menage the whole morning, with groups of five or six riders at a time, teaching them to ride.

'D'you think she'll even have time for mine and Kate's lessons today?' I wondered out loud and then, like she'd heard me, Jane suddenly appeared.

'I've got a free hour at one o'clock, Poppy. We'll do Kate's lesson for the first half, then you can pop onto Kyra for the second.'

Then she was rushing away again before I could even nod.

Chloe was grinning at me. 'Happy now?'

I made a whatever face at her, then couldn't help grinning as well. 'I'd better go and tell Kate.'

I checked my phone.

12.01

An hour to get ready. Actually not that much time.

I found Kate working in Bella's stable and hurried her down to the paddocks.

Kate skipped along beside me. 'It's great not having Allie around.'

'Should you be so happy?' I tried to sound disapproving. 'She might be in a lot of pain.'

'I hope so!'

'Kate!'

The little girl gave me a defiant glance. 'She's been horrible to me.'

How could I answer that?

'Bella!' Kate shouted when we got to the paddocks, forgetting about everything else the instant she saw her pony.

Bella was looking over the fence of the front section of the first paddock.

I knew Kyra was in the second paddock. 'I'll go and get Kyra, will you be okay?'

'Duh! I used to do everything on my own before you started helping.' She laughed and pretended to push me away down the path towards the second paddock.

She was right, she was much better at this than me. All she'd ever really needed was protecting from those bullies.

When we got back up to the yard we groomed our ponies out in the sun and tacked them up. Then, when it was one o'clock, I put Kyra back into her stable so I could lead Bella to the menage with Kate perched on top of her.

We got there just as Jane opened the gate to let the five people from her 12 o'clock lesson out. I didn't know any of them, but they all smiled as they led their horses past us. Once they were gone, I took Bella into the menage and Jane got started with her lesson.

It went great. But I kind of knew it would. Allie and her friends weren't here. Well, except for Beverley, but she was keeping her head down and getting on with looking after Patch and Blake. And when she wasn't doing that, she had her head in her schoolbooks. She was a real sweat, just like Chloe had said. Imagine doing schoolwork in the summer holidays!

Bella and Kate managed to walk and trot and canter without any problems, and since they didn't need me I wandered back to the menage gate to watch them from there.

Kate's mum was leaning on the gate watching too.

'She's doing so well now,' she looked delighted. 'I don't know how you did it.'

There was no point in telling her Kate's only problem was a bunch of idiots who were spooking her pony. That would've just led to a load of questions and trouble. So, I just said, 'I think she just needed someone in with her for a bit.'

We both watched Kate go round.

My gaze wandered to the fence on the right-hand side of the menage. That was where I'd seen the little person. Maybe I should go over sometime and check for little footprints. But what if someone saw me... how would I explain what I was doing?

After Kate and Bella finished it was my turn for a half hour lesson on Kyra.

It was heaven. Somehow everything seemed much easier the second time around and Jane was very pleased. We stuck to walking and trotting again, but Jane said it wouldn't be long before we could try cantering.

After I'd put Kyra away and rubbed her down, Chloe and I got our lunchboxes and decided to eat in the office for a change.

As we went in Beverley looked up in shock.

'Sorry...' She muttered and gathered her books up into her rucksack.

'You don't have to go,' Chloe told her.

'I've got to do Blake...' She rushed out, flinching as she went past us like we might hit her.

'Poor girl,' I said.

'Whatever!' Chloe came back. 'She hangs out with Allie, remember?'

She dropped down on the old sofa against the wall. 'Anyway, I could get used to having this place to ourselves!'

We settled down to eating our sandwiches. And as usual I shared my KitKat. When we'd finished Chloe turned to face me and asked a question.

'Poppy, could you do me a favour?'

I nodded. 'Yeah, sure.'

'It's a big one.'

'Whatever it is, it'll be fine.'

'Really big.'

I laughed, 'What is it?'

'Well, I've gotta go away in a couple of weeks' time.'

'On holiday?'

'Kinda... I'm doing this... competition thing.'

'What sort of competition?'

She made a twisty type of face. 'You won't take the mickey?'

'Why would I?'

'Everyone always takes the mickey.'

'I won't.'

'It's kickboxing.'

I clamped down a giggle that tried to burst out from deep inside me. 'Okay.'

'It's my dad.' She went on. 'He runs this club and makes me do it.'

'So, where is it? The competition, I mean.'

She shrugged. 'Near Paris somewhere.'

'What, is it, like, a big thing then?'

'Kind of, I s'pose... the European championships.'

'What? That sounds huge. Are you good at it or something?'

'I'm okay...'

'But you must be amazing.'

'I'm fine... but, what's more important is, someone needs to look after Eddie while I'm gone. Would you do it?'

Wow! She was going to trust me with her pony, after only knowing me a week? I took a moment... it would be a lot more work, but it should be okay.

'Sure. I'll do it.'

'Really?'

'Yeah.'

'It'll be for a whole week.'

'That's fine.'

'Thanks. Eddie loves you. And you don't have to actually ride him or anything, 'cos... you know...'

She hesitated so I helped her out. 'I'm rubbish?'

159

She laughed. 'No. You're not rubbish. But you only just started riding, and you're doing really well…. you know… considering.'

'Keep digging, Chloe.'

We both laughed.

'No, I mean it, you are doing well. Really. But no one's needs to ride him, Jane's gonna lunge him every day.'

Just like Jane used to lunge Kyra. I found myself smiling and that glow kicked off inside me again… Jane didn't need to do that anymore now that I was riding Kyra.

That conversation with Chloe set off a nagging worry that bothered me the rest of the day. What if my mum and dad were planning a stupid holiday? Then who'd look after Kyra? And what if it clashed with Chloe being away?

The moment mum arrived that night I asked her. 'Are we going away on holiday this summer?'

She avoided speaking and pretended to concentrate on steering the car out through the bumps and dips of the car park.

'Well?' I prompted as we set off down the lane outside.

And then she launched into a whole 'really sorry, but' routine; what with moving house and dad starting a new job and getting settled, everything had got put on hold. 'So we're not going to be able to get away this year.'

Then she stopped talking and peered across at me. 'You're actually happy about that, aren't you?' She laughed.

I tried to look like I wasn't.

'I told you you'd love it at the stables.'

I hated it when she was smug.

My second week at Windwicche stables kicked off totally differently from the first one. Everything got easier and clicked into more of a routine.

Mum started dropping me off earlier so that me and Kate could take Bella and Kyra down to the paddocks together. After that I usually helped Kate with Bella's stable and we chatted. Then we both moved onto Kyra's stable and did that. Then most days Chloe and me went to the barn and heaved bales up to the yard. And then it was the end of the morning, and time for Kate's lesson with Jane.

After that me and Chloe ate lunch and hung out, either down in the barn or, now Allie wasn't around, in the office.

Then, in the afternoon, I got Kyra in from the paddock and groomed her the way Jane had taught me, and then tacked her up ready for my lesson.

That was my favourite part of the day. Jane got me to do a bit more each time, although she said she was taking everything slow but sure. 'If you get the basics right, the harder stuff will be much easier.'

Even so, she had me cantering by the end of that week.

The hot weather finally broke at the start of the third week. On Monday morning mum dropped me off in a torrential storm. I splashed through the car park and down the path to the stable yard with one of dad's old kagouls over my head.

I saw Chloe sheltering under the overhang of roof next to Eddie's stable.

'Wow! Proper boots now,' she laughed as I joined her.

I glanced down. At the weekend mum had forced me to take a couple of hours off to go to a riding shop. I'd come out with two pairs of black riding leggings and some short leather boots with elastic sides. Today was the first time I'd worn them. No way I was ever going to post a picture of me wearing this stuff on Snapchat, but the boots really worked in this weather, and I was hoping the leggings would be less painful than jeans for riding in.

The weather was bad all week and that meant more people hung out in the office, and I started to get to know some of them.

Jenny and Jim were a couple in their thirties who came down at weekends and on weekday evenings. They fussed around their horse, a big bay called Dillon, and talked about getting him ready for jumping competitions. But Chloe said they never went to any. They were nice though.

Heather was really shy and came to the stables every day but didn't have a horse, which was a shame because she was horse mad, but Jane paid her to look after the horses she used for giving lessons and ride them if they needed exercise. She looked older than me and Chloe, probably fifteen, and she was dead quiet. Although Chloe said she was getting chattier now Allie wasn't around.

Teagan and Megan were only little, maybe seven or eight. They ran everywhere, giggling and laughing, and hung out with each other all the time. They had little dappled ponies in stables next door to each other; Prinny and Teddy. And Chloe said Teagan's mum turned up with a trailer attached to her car once a week to take them to Pony Club.

And of course, Beverley was in the office a lot too. She slowly stopped acting like me and Chloe were about to attack her, but she still didn't speak much, and spent most of her time reading her books.

Me and Kate still had our lessons even though it was wet, although a lot of people cancelled out of Jane's regular lessons. At one point when water was dripping down my neck as I trotted around the menage I asked why it didn't have a roof over it. Jane smiled like she was remembering something nice. 'There used to be a good reason for not having a roof, but...' And she glanced up at wet sky. 'Maybe it would be a good idea now.'

Kate and Bella were having a great time in their lessons, although I wondered how long that would last. Allie would come back eventually and everything might just go back to normal. One day, after a lesson, I asked Jane how Allie's leg was doing.

'Her dad emailed. She'll need to keep the cast on for four weeks,' she said.

I tried to work that out... it meant she might be back for the last week of the summer holidays. Not good.

Allie coming back, the end of the summer holidays, and starting at a new school... it was all like a bank of thunderclouds piling up on the horizon.

In no time it was Chloe's last day before going away.

She spent the whole day telling me stuff about Eddie that she'd told me a hundred times already.

'I'll be fine,' I told her. 'And if I need help, I can ask Jane.'

And then, just like that, it was the end of the day and we were hugging and she was driving off in her mum's car.

That night I sat on my bed with my phone. Me and Chloe had set up our own Snapchat and she'd sent me a picture of her packed suitcase, saying they were leaving first thing in the morning.

Seefa was sitting on my bed with me, so I sent Chloe a picture of her.

I got back a 😺 emoji.

'What am I going to do for a whole week without Chloe?' I asked Seefa.

She just sat there and purred.

The next day was a Saturday and the first day I had to look after Eddie on top of everything else.

The sun had come out again and the stables were really busy. People seemed to be in my way the whole time as I rushed around trying to get everything done.

And as usual during the weekend, Jane wanted to squash Kate's and my lessons into the gap between one and two o'clock!

I was exhausted at one o'clock when I arrived at the menage gate with Kate and Bella. Kate's mum smiled at me and I gave her a just-made-it look.

Then I froze when I heard a horrible sound; a chorus of laughter drifting out from the office.

It couldn't be? Could it?

'Can you hold Bella for a second?' I asked Kate's mum.

I stalked down the path next to the office and went in through the open door.

'Hi Poppy,' sneered Allie. 'Bet you're glad I'm back.'

She was sitting on the sofa with one leg up on a chair in a long plastic boot. On either side of her were Gemma and Kim, their smirks mirroring Allie's. And perched on a chair against the far wall, her face pale like she'd seen a ghost, was poor Beverley.

I shrugged. 'I'm not really bothered either way.'

I wasn't ready for this conversation. I hadn't expected to see Allie for another week or more at least. What was she doing here? It wasn't like she could do any work, or ride, or anything.

167

Through the windows I could see the horses from Jane's previous lesson filing out of the menage. Kate would walk in at any moment. What if this lot were here to spook Bella again?

'Just gotta do something...' I rushed back out of the office.

Kate and her mum looked at me expectantly when I reached the menage gate.

'Listen,' I told them. 'Kate's done really well for two weeks now. I think she can go in on her own today.'

Kate beamed, but her mum looked nervous.

'It'll be fine, I promise,' and I turned and rushed away.

Allie and her friends weren't expecting me back again, and they all looked up guiltily as I came through the office door.

Beverley was on the sofa as well now, squashed in between Allie and Gemma. She had her rucksack on her lap and her hand inside it, like she was looking for one of her schoolbooks.

'I think I'll watch from in here,' I said, leaning my butt on the edge of Jane's desk and facing them.

'Get out,' snapped Allie.

'No. I'm staying.'

Gemma and Kim pushed up onto their feet, then waited for Allie to tell them what to do.

I stared at them. Let them try to chuck me out. I wasn't leaving without a fight, and if that happened Jane and everyone else would see.

I was shaking inside, but I knew if I stood my ground, they wouldn't be able to spook Bella.

'F'God's sake!' Allie moaned at last. 'Get me out of here!' She reached out with her hands so Gemma and Kim could pull her up.

She grabbed two crutches from where they were leaning against the tea table and started peg-legging her way out.

As she swung past me, she hissed. 'Just wait 'til I get this boot off, new girl.'

Then she was hobbling out through the office door and away down the path outside, with Gemma and Kim following her.

Beyond them I could see Kate and Bella in the menage, just starting to trot.

'I can't believe you did that,' someone whispered.

I glanced down and found Beverley staring up at me.

She still looked pale and her bottom lip was trembling, but not like she was about to cry or anything, more like she had a chill that was shaking her whole body.

I looked up after Allie and her two friends – did I need to be worried about them? On impulse I asked Beverley. 'Could they still do anything to spook Bella?'

I expected her to act innocent and say... 'what are you talking about?'... or, 'how could anyone be that horrible?'... or, 'we never spooked Bella'.

But what she actually said was. 'No. Not on their own. They're too stupid.'

When I went to get Kyra for my lesson I took a quick look around for Allie, Gemma and Kim, but there was no sign of them anywhere.

I didn't have much time and got Kyra ready as quick as I could then led her to the menage. As I got there Kate was just coming out and gave me a big smile. Thank god I'd gone into the office and faced up to those bullies!

Then I led Kyra into the menage and my heart juddered... there was a whole line of small jumps set up down the middle!

Were they there when Kate started her lesson? I was certain they weren't. So had Jane set them up for me?

She didn't mention them as she got me to walk and trot and canter as usual, but I couldn't help keep glancing at them as I went round.

Then right near the end of the lesson she called out to me.

'I've put some jumps up, d'you think you're ready to try some?'

I nodded and went to say 'yes', but it came out as a croak.

First Jane made me practice standing in my stirrups and leaning forwards while Kyra was walking.

'Yes, that's it, get right forwards so you won't get left behind, and give her some rein so she can stretch.'

Once she was happy she told me to trot, then to canter, and then... oh my god... I was turning sharp left at the back end of the menage to come back down the middle... towards the jumps. The first one came up quickly and I leaned forwards and low over Kyra's neck. It was amazing... like flying. She seemed to launch herself into the air and float over the jump. Then her forefeet landed and she hunched into a tight canter again and... one... two... three... we were sailing over the second jump. There was one final jump but Kyra landed with her hindlegs bunched back under here and her head high in the air. I felt out of control and unbalanced, and had an instant to think... go on, or pull out?

Go on!

If that's what Kyra wanted... I leaned forwards and loosened the reins.

She regained her balance and jumped. And this time it really was like flying. She went way higher than the jump and for a moment it felt like she'd keep on going right up into the sky.

But then we landed and went into a tight turn along the front fence and cantered away around the school like we did this every day.

It was just amazing.

If only Chloe had been here to see it.

Now Allie had been back once, I was worried she'd keep turning up, but each day went by and there was no sign of her.

It began to get easier fitting in looking after Eddie. It was more work and more rushing around, but I got into a rhythm. Even so, I was really looking forward to Chloe coming back.

The weather was nice again so most days I went down to the barn to eat my sandwiches on my own. It didn't seem like anyone other than Chloe and me ever went down there.

I remembered Chloe saying, 'They all think magic fairies bring up the hay and straw.'

Magic fairies?

Maybe that's what that little person in the feed store had been. A magic fairy. After all, it had cleaned up all the mess Allie had made for me, and it had helped me out in the menage when it looked like Blake was attacking Bella.

I got out my phone and scanned through the photos. There! I pinched out the photo of black bins lined up in the store, the one with the little face was peering out. It looked shocked, maybe, and young, almost like a small child, but with eyes that looked old somehow. I swiped forwards to the video and made it go through slowly. There were the black bins again, then the small figure jumping out, staring for a moment, and jumping back again.

If it wasn't for this photo and video, I'd be starting to wonder if imagined the little person. But they proved it, the little person really did exist.

But... I'd never seen it again. Why was that?

I'd been in and out of that feed store loads of times since it had helped me, and there'd been no sign of it. I'd even forgotten to be scared of going in there.

I'd have to tell Chloe about it when she came back. And show her the pictures. To see what she thought it was.

A sudden loud sniff sounded behind me.

What was that?

Was there someone else in the barn? Or *something* else?

Another sniff came and then a small wail, like an animal in pain.

I got up slowly and turned round. The noise sounded like it had come from the back of the barn.

The guys who delivered the bales weren't the tidiest in the world. In some places they were stacked five or six high, but mostly they were lying in jumbled heaps.

Anything could be hiding in amongst them.

I crept towards the back, stepping between the bales carefully.

Then.

'Wahhh!' A full blown sob this time. Right in front of me.

Two more steps and I saw who it was, slumped down in a small space between two bales with her rucksack next to her.

'Beverley!' I sighed with relief.

Her head jerked up. She looked awful. Her eyes were swollen and her cheeks were red.

'What's wrong?' I asked.

'Why would you care?' she muttered back.

'Because...' I kept my voice quiet and gentle. 'I don't like seeing anyone upset.'

She just stared at me.

175

'Don't be nice,' she sniffled. 'I don't deserve it.'

'Why not?'

'I've done terrible things.'

'You?'

'Yeah, me.'

'What sort of things?'

She covered her face with her hands. 'Things… that they made me do.'

'You mean Allie and the others?'

She nodded without taking her hands away. 'And they're coming back next week.'

'Next week?'

I'd been hoping they'd stay away longer.

'Allie messaged. Hospital's taking off her boot tomorrow. She's coming back on Monday.'

'No way!'

'Way,' Beverley gave a huge sniff, braced her hands on the bales either side of her, and levered herself up onto her feet. Then she just stood there, hugging her arms around herself. 'So I can't stay here… I won't do it anymore…'

'Do what?'

'The things they make me do.'

'What things?'

She bent down towards her rucksack. I thought she was going to grab it and run, but instead she opened the top and pulled a book out. Not a schoolbook, but something old, with a leather cover. She thrust it into my hands.

It wasn't heavy or light, or thick or thin, but somewhere in between. I stared at the words on its front cover.

Mischievous Magic ~ Hex and Vex

'Where did you get this?'

'Allie said she found it.'

I flicked through the pages and saw familiar looking text and hand-drawn illustrations. It was just like the books in Jane's kitchen.

It fell open naturally at a page near the middle, like it was one that got used a lot.

Arial sparkles

I scanned the text and illustrations. I'd already guessed what the *things* were that Beverley was talking about and this confirmed it. 'Is this what you used to spook Bella?'

She nodded.

'But why do that? Kate's just a little girl.'

'Allie thought it was funny... and, she wanted to practice.'

'Practice for what?'

'Using it in competitions. To put the other horses off.'

No! My mind flew back to the jumps I'd done on Kyra. They'd been amazing, but also kind of terrifying. What would happen to someone if their horse freaked out in the middle of a jump?

But... something didn't make sense. 'If the idea was to spook the other horses, how come it was Allie who got hurt?'

A tear dribbled down the girl's face. 'They think it was my fault. They think I spooked Blake.'

'And did you?'

Beverley's nod was tiny. 'I hate her so much.'

Then she was crying again properly, her shoulders heaving and shaking. I tried to tell her I understood and that Allie was a bully and deserved what she got, but it didn't help. The small girl just stood there and sobbed.

Eventually her sobs died down and she pulled herself up straight again. Her red, swollen eyes locked onto mine and she held out her hand. 'I need the book back.'

Should I give it to her?

'Allie'll kill me if I don't have it.'

She looked so scared, so desperate, that I let her take it.

She crammed it into her rucksack and stumbled away without another word.

9

Playing With Fire

Chloe arrived back the following Saturday afternoon.

I was next to Kyra's stable when I heard her shout from the top of the yard.

'Poppy!'

'Chloe!' I yelled back.

She ran down and I met her halfway in a big hug.

'I didn't expect you 'til tomorrow,' I gasped.

'We got back at lunchtime.'

'Oh my god! I've got so much to tell you.'

'I bet... It feels like I've been away forever!'

'You have!'

She broke away. 'Just let me say hello to Eddie quickly... then we'll go hang out in the barn.'

'He's out in the paddock.'

'Even better, we'll drop by and see him on the way.'

Eddie was really pleased to see Chloe. He was in the back section of the second paddock, and he whinnied and ran to the fence when she called out to him. Then he drooped his head over the fence for her scratch him.

'Hasn't Poppy been looking after you properly?' She cooed.

Very funny.

'He's been getting the best looking after ever... he probably forgot all about you.'

I didn't.

I let out a small gasp, and at the same time saw Chloe's eyes go wide.

A question bubbled out before I could stop it. 'Did you just hear him speak?'

For long seconds she just stared... then, 'Hear who?'

'Eddie...' No point in stopping now. 'Did you hear him say he hadn't forgotten about you?'

'Did you?'

'Yeah.'

'Then... yeah, I s'pose I did too.'

So it wasn't just me! Chloe could hear the horses talking too! 'Oh my god. I've been too scared to tell anyone. I hear them talking all the time.'

'So do I.'

'I thought I was going mad.'

Eddie snorted because Chloe had stopped scratching his nose.

'You think it's just us, or can everyone hear them?'

I shrugged. 'No one's ever said anything about it.'

Eddie got bored and backed away so he could eat some grass, and we headed down to the barn. When we got there, I checked all around in case anyone was lurking at the back again.

'So what's been happening?' Chloe asked once we were sat down on two straw bales.

Where to start?

We'd already confessed to each other we could hear talking horses, why not double down on the weirdness stakes?

'There's a little person living in the feed store.'

She laughed out loud. 'A little person?'

'Yeah.'

Her laughing stuttered to a halt when I didn't join in. 'Wait, you're actually serious?'

'Yeah... and I can prove it.'

I got out my phone and clicked on the photos icon. It came straight up with the shot I took in the feed store.

Chloe peered at the screen. 'Is it, like, a garden gnome someone dumped in there?'

I leaned over and swiped the screen to bring up the video, then made it go through frame by frame.

'Whoah! It moved!' Chloe shivered. 'Is this for real? It's not photo-shopped or anything?'

'I took these when I was cleaning out the feed store, so I'd know how the bins went back. I didn't see it 'til I looked at them later.'

'Creepy.'

'Really creepy. And there's more.'

'More?'

'Whatever it is, it's kind of helped me out. I think it cleared up the feed store for me, after Allie trashed it. And it got rid of Blake somehow, that time he was in the menage.'

Chole had gone back to the first picture and zoomed it right in. 'Are there girl gnomes? 'Cos this looks like a girl.'

'I thought that as well.'

'Have you seen her again since?' Chloe asked.

I shook my head. 'No. It's like she's just disappeared – if I didn't have these pictures, I'd be thinking I'd made her up.'

We both sat in silence and thought about that for a while, until finally Chloe spoke. 'So, thanks for totally spooking me out. What else has been happening?'

'Well, there's Allie,' I groaned. 'She's coming back on Monday.'

'God no.'

'She's been back once already, with Gemma and Kim helping her and a boot-thing on her leg. I think they wanted to spook Bella again, but I did what we said... I went and sat in the office with them.'

Chloe laughed. 'Bet they loved that.'

'Allie yelled at me to get out, then started threatening me.'

'What did she say?'

'Just to watch out once she got her boot off.'

'Not good... and she'll be back in two days.'

'Yeah.'

What would happen then? Surely, they wouldn't try to beat us up?

That thought made my mind jump to Chloe's competition. 'Wait! How did you do with your kickboxing?'

She gave me a funny look. 'Not taking the mickey?'

'No! How was it?'

'I got silver,' her smiled stretched. 'Dad was really happy.'

'That's second place, right?'

She nodded.

'That's so great... Allie'd better watch out.'

Chloe made a not-so-sure face. 'I'm not really meant to get into fights or anything, not outside of the club... I could get banned and then dad would go ballistic.'

'That's not so good.'

'No, but... what the hell... I'm still gonna stick up for you if Allie tries anything funny.'

'Thanks, Chloe.'

'S'what friends are for.'

Friends... that's what me and Chloe were now. Close as any of the friends I left behind.

But it wasn't just getting into fights we had to worry about.

'There's something else that may be a problem.'

'What?'

'I've kind of found out how they're spooking the horses.'

'How?'

'You promise not to laugh?'

'Why would I laugh?'

'Because you'll think it's mad.'

'I promise I won't.'

'They're using magic spells.'

Chloe laughed.

'You promised!' I gasped, but then I was laughing too. Saying it out loud sounded so random.

After a few moments Chloe made her face go serious. 'So... is this like your *little person* thing? Like, do you mean it for real, that they're using magic?'

I nodded. 'Yeah, for real.'

'But how d'you know?'

''Cos Beverley told me.'

'Beverley?'

I told Chloe about finding Beverley in the barn yesterday, and the book of spells she showed me, and how Allie had wanted her to use it to spook the other horses at jumping competitions, but then she'd used it on Allie instead.

'It was Beverley that caused Allie's accident? Way to go! Maybe she's not so bad, after all.'

Chloe was right, but... 'I wish I hadn't given her that book back. Allie might force her to use it on us. She might, like, turn us into frogs or something.'

186

That started off a fit of giggles, but they quickly faltered into silence. What if she could do something like that?

A noise made us look up.

Beverley was at the front of the barn, her rucksack dangling from one hand. How long had she been there?

'Don't worry about eating flies for the rest of your lives... I'm going to leave before Allie comes back.'

'Leave?' I was shocked.

'But what about school?' Chloe asked. 'Allie's still gonna be there.'

Beverley shook her head. 'Mum said we can move house, go somewhere else completely, so I don't have to go back there either.'

God! I knew what it was like to uproot your whole life. 'You shouldn't have to do that. Not because of that bunch of idiots.'

'But if I don't... they're gonna make me do more and more spells... worse and worse things.'

She put down her rucksack and reached inside, and her hand came out holding the leatherbound book.

'Here,' she walked over and dropped it in my lap. 'This stuff is scary. You take it.'

Then she was walking away again, kind of hunched over with her shoulders shaking. She was trying to hold it in, but she couldn't help one sob escaping.

'Are you sure about this?' I called out.

But she didn't stop, just grabbed her rucksack off the ground and ran out of the barn.

'Oh... my... God,' breathed Chloe.

I looked down at the book in my lap. It was the same one Beverley had shown me before. 'What the hell are we going to do with this?'

'It has to be Jane's – shouldn't we give it back to her?'

That was the sensible thing to do. The safe thing to do. Look at how much pain it had put Beverley through.

'I guess so,' I nodded unsurely. 'I wonder if Jane knows this stuff is for real.'

'How could she not?'

Chloe had a point... Jane had loads of books like this. She'd told me she collected them as a hobby, but that didn't seem very likely.

Chloe reached over. 'Can I take a look at it?'

I let her take it.

'Wow!' She breathed as she picked it up. 'It feels alive.'

I watched her trace the words on the cover with one finger, then open the book to the first page. She was being more patient than I'd been, taking it a page at a time.

'It says here it's a book of spells. It's kind of hard to read... d'you think it's handwritten?'

I shifted along the bale so I could look too. The words were very neat – every line straight – every letter consistently sized and shaped.

I shook my head. 'It looks kind of printed... in a weird font.'

My eyes lingered on the first two lines at the top of the page.

DANGER

Magic should only be practiced by those proficient in the art

That seemed pretty clear – we shouldn't be messing with it.

Chloe moved on to the next page.

Transient Aromas.

'This is amazing...' She breathed.

I remembered the name on the front cover – something about mischievous magic – was this a book full of magic practical jokes?

Chloe was muttering to herself, reading aloud, in an odd kind of rhythm that wasn't how she normally spoke.

'What the…?' I put my hands over my mouth and nose and scrambled to my feet. Then I was running, past straw bales to get out into the sunlight, and the fresh air. Chloe was right behind me.

We stopped outside the barn, coughing and spluttering and bent over with our hands braced on our knees.

'Jesus,' Chloe choked out. 'It only bloody works!'

'That was the… worst thing… I've ever smelt.'

'It said… it said it was… dragon vomit.'

Somehow knowing that fact made the last traces of the smell in my nose and mouth even worse.

'Nice choice.'

'The other options were even nastier.'

We slowly recovered. And the implications of what Chloe had just done started to sink in. She'd actually made a magic spell work!

'You know,' I breathed. 'This stuff could be really dangerous.'

'Yeah...' Chloe agreed. 'Let's try another one.'

We spent the rest of the afternoon in the barn. There was nothing urgent that needed doing up in the stables. Eddie and Kyra were happily grazing out in the paddocks, and I'd already mucked out their stables and got their hay and water ready for when we brought them back in.

It turned out the spells worked for me as well.

The first one I tried sounded less horrible than the dragon vomit one.

Illusions to fool the unwary.

I chose it because it looked simple. Some of the spells had a load of stuff you had to get together or hand-drawn pictures of apparatus you had to have. This was just an incantation to speak out loud while you imagined the illusion you wanted to create.

When I finished speaking the words I looked around. Nothing seemed to have happened. Then there was a loud 'meeow' and Seefa walked out from behind a straw bale.

'Aaah,' said Chloe. 'She's cute.'

'She's my cat at home.'

'Then why's she here?'

'It's the spell... she's just an illusion.'

'Oh yeah,' she shook her head. 'My dumb.'

'Do people even say that?'

She shrugged. 'Dunno... they say *my bad.*'

Seefa jumped up onto her hind legs and did a kind of a dance.

Chloe giggled. 'What's she doing?'

'Whatever I want her to do... I just have to think it.'

'Wow.'

Chloe sat forwards so she could poke Seefa with one finger. It went right through her. 'She really isn't there,' she murmured. 'She looks so real... apart from the dancing, that is.'

I laughed and then suddenly she was gone.

'Where'd she go?' Asked Chloe.

'You made me laugh... I stopped concentrating.'

Chloe looked thoughtful for a couple of moments. 'D'you think this is the spell they used to make it look like Blake was in the menage?'

That made sense. 'It must've been.'

We kept trying different spells, sticking to the ones that looked easy. Each time I kept expecting them not to work, but they always did. They were addictive. We kept doing *just one more.*

'What about this?' Chloe suggested.

I remembered the dragon vomit smell. 'Are you sure?'

'All the spells have been pretty silly so far. How bad could tiny dragons be?'

'Last one, then.'

Chloe nodded. 'Last one.'

She started reading the incantation under her breath, and like all the other times her voice suddenly didn't quite sound like her. It went on for a while, then she stopped and looked up. 'See anything?'

'Nope.'

We both looked around. Nothing on the barn floor. Nothing up in air. Chloe sighed. 'Maybe I got it wrong.'

Then something swooped down from the roof of the barn. It didn't fly quite like a bird, more like a bat, except it wasn't black... more bronzy. It flew in jittery circles through the air.

'That's it,' Chloe laughed. 'A tiny dragon.'

'It's kind of cute.'

'Yeah, it is.'

Then it breathed out a small jet of fire.

I gasped. 'It really is a dragon.'

193

It was amazing. It kept on flying around, snapping its little mouth like it was catching bugs out of the air, not seeming to get tired at all.

Then something else came from nowhere and smashed into it.

Another little dragon!

They crashed onto the floor together and rolled apart, then leapt back into the air and started spiralling, firing small jets of fire at each other.

Seconds later another tiny dragon swooped in and joined the fight. Then another... and another.

'Oh no!' Muttered Chloe.

I leaned over and looked at the page open on her lap. 'How do you stop it?'

We both scanned the text frantically. Nothing. I reached down and turned the page. 'There!' I pointed. The spell had gone on to the next page, and at the end was a final short incantation.

Chloe read it out, not muttering this time.

Above us more and more dragons kept appearing, all fighting each other and jetting out breaths of fire, their tiny roars combining to create an screechy din.

Chloe read the last word of the incantation and we both looked up.

The tiny dragons kept fighting.

'There!' I shouted. One of the dragons had popped out of existence.

'And there!' Chloe had seen another one go.

Over the next minute the swarm of dragons shrank to nothing. With a tiny roar of protest the last one disappeared.

And everything went quiet.

'Bloody hell,' Chloe breathed. 'D'you think they're all gone?'

'I hope so.'

Chloe slammed the book shut. 'That was definitely the last spell.'

'Definitely. But... the last one for today, or forever?'

By the look on her face Chloe was thinking the same thing.

'We really should give the book back to Jane,' I said.

Chloe made a do-we-have-to face.

'I get what you're saying,' she said. 'But what about Allie and her friends?'

'What d'you mean?'

'Well, we don't really know how that's all going to work out. Suppose we need something else... like an edge... to use against them?'

She could be right. Allie had already threatened me. And school started in a couple of weeks, where she had an even bigger gang. Maybe these spells could come in useful... but should we even go there?

'I don't know.'

'Me neither,' Chloe agreed. 'Let's leave it 'til tomorrow and decide then.'

10

The Worst Day Ever… again

That evening at 7.50pm was when I got the message from Chloe.

Pls come down. Really need your help. Now. 🙏

I knew she was still at the stables. She'd told me earlier that her mum wasn't picking her up 'til 8pm, because she was busy getting unpacked from their trip.

I ran downstairs to where mum and dad were watching Strictly. 'Something's happened at the stables, Chloe needs me down there now!'

They both gave me a not-a-chance look. So I begged. Then they asked if I'd tried to call or message Chloe back. And I said that I had, but her phone just kept ringing and the message I'd sent was showing as unread.

'I know what you girls are like,' mum said. 'It'll be nothing.'

And I shouted that Chloe wasn't like my old friends, and that it wouldn't be nothing. Then they told me off for shouting, and I said sorry, and then I begged some more. I must've got through to them, or they just decided it was the only way to shut me up, because we all ended up in the car driving to the stables at just gone 8.15pm.

The drive there was a nightmare. With a cold weight inside telling me something awful had happened at the stables, made worse when the fire engine overtook us and we had to follow it all the way there.

Then we arrived and Chloe ran across the carpark outlined by the flames leaping up into the sky and sobbed, 'What have we done?'...and I knew exactly what she meant. Because it wasn't the stables that were on fire, it was the barn... where we'd been doing those spells all that afternoon, one of which had created the swarm of tiny dragons, all fighting each other with little jets of flame.

'Calm down, girls. Don't worry. No-one's in any danger.' Jane's steady voice came from close by and made us both jump. 'It's just the barn that's gone up, and the firemen are running a hose down there now.'

Oh god! What should we say to her?

'But it was our fault,' blurted Chloe.

'Your fault?' Jane's look became stern. 'I'll be very cross if you girls have been smoking down in that barn.'

We both shook our heads at that.

'Vaping then,' Jane went on. 'I heard it on the radio... those disposable vapes have batteries that start fires.'

Chloe made a 'yuck' face. 'We don't smoke or vape.'

Jane looked confused. 'So, why do you think it's your fault?'

I glanced at Chloe and found her looking at me. We'd planned to talk to Jane anyway... about the spell book... and about everything else. But now?

I took a deep breath to start talking... but then another voice cut in.

'How awful, Jane... are the horses all right?' It was mum.

Jane whispered. 'We'll talk about this later.' Then her attention shifted away to my mum.

'Yes, they're all fine. The fire's in the barn, Mrs Carter, which is a long way from the stables.'

Jane steered mum away, leaving Chloe and me on our own.

199

'Oh my god!' I whispered. 'She looked really cross.'

Chloe nodded. 'She's gonna kill us.'

We didn't get a chance to talk to Jane again that night. She was busy with the firemen and signing bits of paper and god knows what and both of our mums wanted to get us back home.

All the way back mum and dad kept saying things like 'the main thing is no-one got hurt'... and 'it's good the barn was so far from the stables'... and 'I wonder what caused it?'

They were dialling up the being-jolly factor to ten, probably because I looked upset and they were trying to cheer me up. But that was never going to work because I was actually more terrified than upset.

What would Jane say when we told her what we'd done? And would she think it was me who stole the book, since she'd already caught me looking through one?

Everything kept running round in my head; me and Chloe playing with the spell book, the tiny dragons in the barn, the crackling tongues of fire licking the dusk sky and, always, coming back to it again and again, the furious expression on Jane's face.

It wouldn't even stop when I went to bed. Seefa sensed something was wrong and cuddled up by my pillow. But even her tiny purrs in my ear didn't help.

11

Wicches

The alarm on my phone went off and I opened my eyes.

For a few moments it felt just like any other day; staring up at my flaky, cracked bedroom ceiling; listening to mum clattering downstairs in the kitchen.

Then what happened last night came crashing back in on me.

'Oh no...' I groaned.

I jumped out of bed and ran to the shower. I couldn't be late today or Chloe would to have to face Jane on her own.

'Why the rush?' Mum asked when I jumped down the stairs two at a time. 'Will they even want you at the stables until they've cleaned up?'

'I just need to get there, Mum.'

Twenty minutes later mum had dropped me off.

'Hi Poppy,' Chloe had been waiting in the car park for me.

'Hi Chloe.'

'Jane said we have to go into her house.'

'You've seen already?'

Chloe nodded.

'What was she like?'

Chloe made her twisty face. 'A bit serious.'

I glanced over at Jane's house. 'Better go in, then.'

The back door was closed when we got to it. I knocked and for a moment there was silence. Maybe she wasn't there... maybe we could just go down to the yard and start work like normal.

Then footsteps sounded inside and the door clicked and opened.

'Okay, come in you two!' Jane sounded stern.

We followed her to the breakfast bar and sat down on two of the stools. She sat opposite and her eyes flicked between us. 'So, what was it? Smoking or vaping?'

'We already said, we don't do either!' Chloe insisted.

'No we don't!' I agreed.

'So, what then?'

Chloe reached inside her coat and pulled out the leather covered spell book. She placed it in front of Jane on the worksurface.

Jane stared at it. I could almost hear her brain switching gears. Her face went from confusion, to surprise, to annoyance, then back to confusion again.

203

'You found my missing book?' She said finally.

Chloe and I both nodded.

Jane picked it up, looked at the front and back covers, then flicked through the pages inside.

'It's actually quite valuable.' She hesitated for a moment. 'Or it used to be, when it was good for anything.'

I glanced at Chloe. I wasn't sure what to say next, and it looked like she was the same.

Jane put the book down. 'Well, it's good to get it back, but what does it have to do with the fire?'

My mind flashed back to the first time I'd seen the book, when I'd found Beverley crying in the barn. That seemed a good place to start – at least it would make it clear up front that I hadn't stolen her book.

Jane listened as I told her about Beverley, and how she was being forced to do spells by Allie, and then how she'd told me and Chloe she was going to leave the stables and given us the book. Then I got to the bit I was dreading, telling Jane how we'd tried out some of the spells in the barn.

I glanced up to see how cross she was, but she was just smiling and shaking her head. 'I know it's fun to think that magic spells are real,' she said gently. 'But there is no magic, Poppy, not anymore.'

Chloe and I shared a glance.

Then Chloe picked up where I left off. 'We should've brought the book straight back to you,' she said. 'And we shouldn't have tried any spells, especially that tiny-dragon one. But they did work, Jane, they really did.'

'There's no need to make stuff up, girls,' Jane came back. 'I can put your minds at rest. The firemen found a firework, a cheap little rocket thing, burnt out near the front of the barn. They said it happens a lot, all year round, not just at Guy Fawkes anymore.'

Oh.

I glanced at Chloe and saw her shoulders had relaxed. She caught my eye and gave a little smile.

The fire wasn't our fault after all!

But...

'We're not making stuff up,' I stated. 'Chloe's right, the spells do work.'

'Okay,' said Jane, turning the book towards me and opening it at a random page. 'Show me. That's a simple one... make it work.'

I peered at the page. It was the spell I'd used to make Seefa appear in the barn.

'Go on,' Chloe muttered.

I nodded and pulled the book closer, then read the incantation under my breath.

I finished and nothing happened.

Long seconds went by and Jane smiled at me kindly. 'Life just isn't like in Harry Potter...'

A meow drifted up from the floor and a small black cat jumped up onto the breakfast bar.

'Oh my goodness,' Jane breathed.

The cat stood up on its hind legs and started to dance. Jane reached out to touch it and her fingers went right through.

'My goodness... oh my goodness,' she muttered and ran across the kitchen to the back door. She opened it wide and stood there pulling in deep breaths and staring out at nothing.

'How could I not have seen?' She muttered. 'How could I not have sensed it?'

She closed the door and came back to us.

'So, are you three?"

'Three what?' I asked.

'A coven of three,' she shook her head like she couldn't believe what she was saying. 'The first new coven for... I don't know, a hundred years, maybe more.'

Nothing she was saying made any sense, but one thing she'd got wrong for sure. 'There's only two of us, Chloe and me.'

And then there was a knock at the door. Not loud, more like a mouse had ran into it, but it still made us all look round.

The door opened slowly and a head peeked in. 'Is anybody here?'

It was Beverley.

Beverley looked at me, then at Chloe, then finally fastened her eyes on Jane.

'Mum said to give you this.' She walked forwards holding out a white envelope in one trembling hand. 'It's got a cheque to pay for full livery for Patch, until we can find a new place for him, when we know where we've moved to.'

'You can't leave, Beverly,' Jane stated it like a fact, her face flat, free of its normal smile.

'But I have to...'

'You can't.' Jane made no attempt to take the envelope, and instead stood up and placed her hands on the girl's shoulders. 'You are three now; you, Poppy, and Chloe. You can't run away from it. And what you'll need to face in the future will be far worse than any problems you think you have now.'

I glanced at Chloe and she was giving me the same look back. What would we need to face in the future?

'Three what?' Managed Beverley.

'You are a coven of three,' Jane whispered, as though that explained everything. And then she suddenly pulled Beverley into a hug.

The girl seemed to sag into her arms.

'You're so young,' Jane murmured. Then she broke out of the hug and turned to glance back at us. 'You're all so young.'

Jane kept one arm around Beverley's shoulders and guided her towards a wooden door that must lead deeper into the house.

'Come on... all of you. I need to tell you a story.'

The door opened onto a small snug, with a TV in the corner and a sofa and a comfy looking armchair. Jane sat us on the sofa and then slumped into the armchair.

'So, you know that magic is real.'

It wasn't a question, but I found myself nodding anyway. Either side of me Chloe and Beverley were doing the same.

'I thought it was gone,' she went on. 'It was meant to be gone... sucked away into a hole in the earth and sealed up tight so it could never come back.'

'Why?' I found myself asking.

'I'll get to that,' Jane whispered. 'But first you need to know what it was like before. History has been rewritten and most people who would remember are gone. Only myths and legends remain that hint of what the world was once like.'

This was getting weird. 'Are you saying all the stuff we're learning at school is wrong?'

'No... not wrong... but anything, everything, about magic, and the fact that it was real, has been taken out.'

'Why?'

Jane shrugged. 'We thought it was best. Or people would just search forever to find it again. It's human nature.'

So many questions were zinging around in my head that I couldn't focus on just one.

'It was wonderful, though,' Jane went on. 'Light and bright and exciting and dangerous. All the magical creatures you've ever heard of, good and bad, really lived. This world is a pale shadow of what it once was.'

Beverley found her voice, although it was weak and jittery still. 'You mean fairies, and elves, and all that stuff?'

Jane nodded. 'Fairies, elves, gnomes, unicorns, dragons, ogres... everything.'

'What about people?' I found myself asking. 'How did people live with all of those... things?'

'People...' Jane started. 'Humans... whatever you want to call us... we were the most, and the least, magical of all.'

'How do you mean?'

'Every person had a little magic in them, enough to do everyday spells. But a few were much better, more powerful.'

That made sense. At my old school there'd been a few people who were great at sport, and there'd been the sweats who aced all the academic stuff... but most people had been kind of average at everything, me included.

'And of them all, the wicches were the most powerful,' Jane went on.

Did she say *witches*? Because she said it a bit strangely, like *wik-ches*.

'Especially when they were joined in a coven.' Her glance swept across us. 'Like you three.'

Us three? Jane thought we were, how had she said it, wicches?

'But we just read out a few spells from a book,' Chloe said. 'We're not, like, good at it or anything.'

Jane shook her head. 'Now you've woken me up to it, I can feel the magic in the air outside. But it's tenuous, vague... hardly there at all. It could even just be... a final eddy or something... that never drained away. The fact that you girls can make any spells work at all makes you very talented indeed.'

Her eyes focussed on Beverley. 'I sense you are the most skilled, and that you could eventually master even the most complex spells.'

That kind of fitted, since Beverley always had her head in her schoolbooks.

Jane turned to Chloe next. 'And you seem to have raw power, that Beverley can shape and use when you perform spells together.'

That made Chloe smile and go red.

Finally, Jane looked at me. 'And Poppy, you're a good all-rounder.'

The story of my life!

'So, what you said about it being a final eddy type thing,' Chloe asked. 'Does that mean the magic here could all just... drift away?'

Disappointment made me go still inside. What if Chloe was right? The idea of being able to do magic, of being a wicche, felt so exciting, so special.

Jane was shrugging. 'I don't know, Chloe. But we must find out. Because, if the magic's really coming back, it's going to change everything. There was a good reason we drained it away.'

'What was that?' Beverley asked. She sounded scared.

'That's a much longer story, and we don't have time for it now. You all have work to do, your horses will wonder where you are. And I need to contact some people… tell them what's happening here… and find out if they've seen anything like it where they are.'

'Other wicches?' I asked.

Jane nodded. 'Yes, other covens. And if I can, the Grand Coven itself.'

'And will you use magic to do that?'

'In a way…' Jane smiled. 'Modern magic… email and the internet conference calls.'

She walked us back into the kitchen and out through her back door. We all had more questions, but she shushed us. 'Later…' She said.

When we got outside she focused on Beverley.

'Is your mum waiting in the carpark?' She asked.

Beverley nodded. 'Yes.'

'We'll need to speak to her, to tell her you want to stay after all.'

Beverley looked unsure and Jane stopped us all halfway down the path, taking the small girl by the shoulders again and looking deep into her eyes.

'You're part of a team now, a sisterhood as old as time, and the three of you can stand against anyone... especially a bunch of non-magical bullies.'

What? Jane had known what Allie and her friends were like all along?

Beverley glanced first at Chloe and then at me, her eyes questioning. Chloe stepped up and put an arm round her shoulders. 'Jane's right, we're a team, from now on we stick up for each other.'

I stepped up to the other side of Beverley and hugged her close as well. I was going to say the same as Chloe, but suddenly my throat tightened, and my eyes welled up. 'What she said,' I just about managed.

I felt Beverley's trembling shoulders become steadier.

'Okay,' she said to Jane. 'Let's go and tell mum.'

Beverley was back down in the yard twenty minutes later.

Chloe and me were coming back from the paddocks when we saw her outside Patch's stable. We rushed over.

'Was your mum okay?' I asked.

Beverley nodded. 'I think she was relieved.'

'What did you say to her?' Chloe asked.

'It was Jane who told her.' She looked tearful again, even though she was smiling too. 'She said I'd made some really close friends here, and that they'd promised to look after me so I wouldn't be bullied anymore.'

And suddenly we were all in a group hug. And my eyes were stinging again. And I even heard a sniffle from Chloe.

When we broke apart our smiles all mirrored each other.

'All for one, eh?' Said Chloe, putting her hand out palm down.

'And one for all…' I finished the cheesy saying and put my hand on top of hers.

Then Beverley put her hand of top of mine.

We stayed like that for a few seconds, grinning like idiots, then instinctively threw our hands up in the air and fluttered our fingers like they were birds flying away.

That set off a fit of giggles that made everyone nearby look round.

It took us a while to recover but when we did, we decided we needed to get on with our work. Bev, which was what she insisted we call her from now on, took Patch out to the paddocks, while me and Chloe made a start on mucking out.

Around mid-morning I'd just finished Kyra's stable when a noise made me glance out through the open door. The stables were just as crowded as a normal Sunday despite the fire, and so there'd been loads of people about in the yard all morning, but now they all seemed to be walking up towards the carpark.

I put down my fork and went out into the sunshine. What was going on? I started following them and as I went past Patch's stable Bev looked over the door. 'What's happening?' She called out.

'Don't know... let's go and see.'

As we reached the path to the carpark the noise of running feet came up behind us. 'Wait for me,' puffed Chloe.

We followed the short path to the car park and came to a stop at the back of a small crowd of people. We edged around them until we reached the fence along the side of Jane's garden, where we could see better.

'Back a bit… back a bit…' A man with a yellow coat was standing behind a big lorry waving it towards him. 'Okay, stop!'

There was a hiss of brakes and the lorry stopped, about halfway down the carpark, next to a large plastic sheet that had been laid out of the ground.

'Hay and straw delivery… that makes sense,' Chloe muttered.

We'd gone and looked at the barn earlier that morning and it had been a blackened wreck. There'd be no point trying to store anything down there until it had been cleaned up and rebuilt.

The driver of the lorry and another man jumped out, and then all three of them started unloading bales. 'Straw at the back, hay in the front!' Ordered the one in the yellow jacket.

They started piling bales on the plastic sheet.

'Hello, you three,' a voice came from behind us. It was Jane.

I looked round to see if her expression was smiling or serious. It turned out it was somewhere in-between.

'Come inside for a moment,' she said and walked back towards her house.

We glanced at each other, then climbed over her fence and followed.

Once we were inside her kitchen, she closed the door behind us.

'I've got some conference calls set up for later this afternoon.' she started. 'But I realised I needed to talk to you before I get caught up in them... about Allie.'

'What about her?' Bev asked, her voice starting to shake again.

'She's due back tomorrow, probably with those awful friends she drags around with,' Jane confirmed what we already knew. 'But, if you want, I can ring Allie's parents today and tell them she's banned from the stables, and that they'll need to move Blake somewhere else.'

'You'd do that?'

Jane nodded. 'Their behaviour's been even worse than I realised. And you three are my priority now. What do you want me to do?'

Chloe and I both turned to Bev. 'What do you think?' I asked her.

'I think...' Bev said slowly, then took a deep breath and forced the shake out of her voice. 'That banning her will just make things worse when we go back to school.' She stood up tall and straightened her shoulders. 'And anyway, I'm going to have to face her sometime, it might as well be now.'

'Way to go!' Congratulated Chloe. 'We'll be there for you.'

'Yeah, we will,' I joined in.

'So, you're all sure about that?' Jane looked at each of us in turn.

We all nodded.

'Excellent!'

She rushed us out of the kitchen.

'Well done, girls,' she called after us as we walked away down her path. 'It's good to start facing your fears. God knows, Allie won't be the scariest thing you'll come up against if you're right about the...' And she dropped to a loud whisper, '...magic coming back.'

And she pressed the door shut.

What?

When we got back down into the yard, I saw little Kate waiting for me down by Kyra's stable.

'Poppy!' She called out and ran up to meet me.

I felt instantly guilty. What with everything going on, I'd completely forgotten about working with Kate and Bella this morning.

She hugged me around my waist. 'I've got my lesson in half an hour.'

I hugged her back. 'I'll come and help with Bella.'

Thirty minutes later I led Bella, with Kate on top, into the menage.

Jane was already standing in the middle and called out to me. 'Why don't you get Kyra ready so you can have your lesson after Kate?'

I glanced up at Kate. 'Will you be okay?'

"Course I will, silly!'

I shut the menage gate and ran down to the paddocks. I found Kyra waiting with her head hung over the fence, like she'd known I was coming to get her. I clipped a rope onto her head collar and jogged back to the yard, then groomed her quickly and got her tacked up.

I made it back to the menage just as Kate and Bella were coming out.

'Was your lesson okay?' I asked, already knowing it had been by the little girl's smile.

'Great!'

I led Kyra into the menage and shut the gate behind me, then hauled myself up onto her back.

Then I noticed there were jumps set up in the menage again. But not just down the middle this time. There were loads, and they were all over the menage at odd angles. A thrill ran down the back of my neck and all the way to my toes.

Jane called out. 'I thought we'd try some jump combinations. I want to know how your balance is getting on.'

Something about the way she said it made me wonder *why* she wanted to know.

First of all, she got me and Kyra to walk and trot and canter, just like normal. Kyra was so good, I hardly had to kick her or anything, she always seemed to know what I wanted her to do. Ten minutes later Jane got us to stop and came over. 'Hop down and follow me.'

I dropped down to the ground and led Kyra by her reins as Jane showed us each of the jumps in turn.

'When you're in a jumping competition, all the riders get to walk the course, so they can remember which way to go and take a look at the jumps.'

She took us between the jumps twisting right and left and sometimes just going straight on.

Finally, she stopped and looked at me. 'So that's five jumps, do you think you can remember the course?'

My brain was buzzing with images of blue and white poles, and red and white poles, and double jumps and single jumps. But I thought I'd got it. I nodded.

'Great... hop back on then.'

She got me to canter around the outside of the menage once more, then shouted, 'Okay, Poppy, first jump!'

Kyra turned in sharply from the far end of the menage and headed for the first jump. I hadn't even told her to do that!

'Get forward!' Jane shouted. But I was already out of the saddle and leaning over Kyra's neck.

I hardly felt the first jump, Kyra was so smooth.

The next was straight ahead, and three paces later we were flying over that too.

Then we twisted left. Two choppy paces and I got thrown slightly backwards as Kyra seemed to take off vertically to make a high single jump. Then she cantered diagonally across the menage, doubling back through the gap between the first two jumps, then turned sharp right for a wide double. Kyra gathered herself for that one, and I made sure I leaned right forwards. The power when she took off was breath-taking. Kyra easily cleared the jump and turned right almost the moment her hooves touched the ground. There was just one last jump, which was right next to the second jump we did, but one bar higher. It looked huge. Kyra's canter went choppy again and the final jump came up slowly... then, oh my god! We were shooting up like a rocket... I was sure I'd got my position right but I still felt like I was going to fall off... but an instant later we were coming down again and I had to fling myself back so I didn't go over Kyra's neck. Then we'd landed and were cantering easily back down towards the menage gate.

I heard cheers from inside the office and glanced over to see Chloe and Bev standing up and looking through the windows and waving their hands.

'Well done, Poppy!' Jane shouted. 'You aced it!'.

223

That afternoon limped by like a tortoise with a bad leg. I thought it would never end. I kept bumping into Chloe, then Bev, then Chloe, then Bev, and each time we rehashed variations of the same questions... how d'you think Jane's calls are going?... are we really wicches?... what's going to happen when Allie comes back?

It wasn't until early in the evening that we saw Jane again. She appeared at end of the path from the car park and beckoned for us to come up to her house.

She sat us all down in her snug again.

'What did you find out?' I blurted.

Jane shrugged. 'Not much, I'm afraid.'

Chloe took over. 'What did all the other... wicches... say?'

'The Grand Coven granted me an audience,' and Jane made a face like that was amazing. 'And they asked me loads of questions... especially about the three of you... but then they said they'd seen no evidence of any magic coming back and that I was jumping at shadows.'

'And that's it?'

'I suggested someone should go and check the seal... but the Magister said it would be a waste of time.'

'Who's the Magister?' I asked.

'The leader of the Grand Coven.'

Bev cut in. 'Couldn't we just show this, Magister person, some magic, like, actually working?'

Jane frowned. 'I suggested that too... but she said I was being ridiculous and I must be mistaken about there being a new coven and she had no more time to waste.'

Jane was quiet for a few moments, then she spoke again in a whisper. 'And she's meant to be my sister...' Her fingers reached to touch an old golden locket that hung round her neck on a chain.

'Your sister?'

'We were three once, just like you, our own small coven. Beatrice, who's now the Magister, myself and poor Cassiopea.'

The way she said 'poor Cassiopea' was really sad, and she clutched the locket tight.

'Did something happen to Cassiopeia?' I asked.

Jane smiled weakly. 'She was the brightest of us, the cleverest, the most powerful... and that was her downfall.'

'Downfall?'

'She went quite mad. Maybe delving too deep into the high magic did it. She decided the world needed to change, that it should be ruled by a single person, who knew what was best for everyone. Her.'

'What happened?' Bev asked.

'She made an orb,' Jane held up her hands like she was holding something about the size of a netball. 'That could suck magic in until it became horrendously powerful. Then she threatened to use it against any country that didn't submit to her army of magical beasts.'

'And did that work?'

'No. We found a way to stop her. One she didn't expect. We drained all the magic out of the world and took away her power.'

'So why is it coming back now?' Bev asked. 'What does that mean?'

'Well, back when we were about to seal the magic away in a hole deep in the earth, Cassiopeia came to us and begged that we stop. When we refused, she made a binding vow and threw herself into the hole. It was terrible.'

'What's a binding vow?' I asked.

'A magical promise. She vowed to return and bring the magic with her.'

We all went quiet. In my head I was seeing a dark enclosed place made of jagged rock, with a big hole in the floor surrounded by figures in black capes, chanting words of a powerful spell while a tragic, beautiful heroine sacrificed herself to save the magic from leaving the world.

'So does that mean Cassiopeia's coming back too?' Bev asked.

That didn't sound good. A crazy wicche rising from the dead and bringing a world's worth of magic with her!

Jane finally stopped fiddling with her locket and leaned towards us. 'I don't know. But someone needs to check if the magic's really coming back. And it looks like it's going to have to be us.'

'How do we do that?' I asked, not sure I really wanted to know the answer.

'The seal is in Woolly Hole – we just need to go there to see if it's still intact.'

Woolly hole? That name seemed familiar. 'Isn't that a load of caves or something?'

Jane nodded. 'Yes. The other side of the country. And to get there, I think I'll need your help.'

She glanced at each of us in turn. I found myself nodding when she looked at me, even though I had no idea what sort of help she wanted.

'That's settled then,' she said finally. 'And I must say you're all being incredibly brave.'

Were we? What had we just agreed to?

Jane kept talking. 'Let's try it tomorrow night. Do you think your parents would agree to a sleepover?'

12

Allie's Return

I'd expected mum and dad to need some convincing about the sleepover.

But they'd both said fine, and that it was nice I was making friends, and mum helped me get my stuff together.

I messaged Chloe and Bev to say it had been easy-peasy... and they came back saying their parents had been the same.

Next morning mum dropped me off at the stables with a couple of bags full of way too much stuff. I had enough for a whole week's trip! I took the bags straight to Jane's house and dropped them in her kitchen. There was a pile of bags already there – it looked like Chloe and Bev had nearly as much stuff as me.

After that I headed down to the yard, with little flying bugs jittering around in my tummy. Allie was due back today. And the last time I'd seen her she'd threatened me.

'Hey, new girl!'

The bugs went into a frenzy. Allie was down near the bottom of the yard. Wait! She was right next to Kyra's stable.

The bugs got killed by a chill that shivered through me... she'd better not have done anything to Kyra!

I felt like running down to check the pony was okay... but that was probably what Allie wanted, so I just lengthened my strides to get down there as quick as I could.

As I got close, I saw Kyra was perfectly fine, munching away at her hay inside her stable. I tried not to look relieved in the face of Allie's smirky glare.

'I'm hardly the *new girl* anymore.'

'Naw... I can see,' she looked me up and down. 'You're all stabled-up now.'

'What are you doing next to Kyra's stable?'

'Just came to say hello,' Allie glanced behind her. 'But that pony's mental, she tried to bite me.'

I couldn't help a smile twitching my lips.

Allie gave me a nasty look. 'Yeah, laugh it up, new girl... you won't be doing it for long.'

She turned and slouched away towards the office. She looked even bigger than the last time I saw her. The jitters started up again inside me. Maybe we should've got Jane to ban her from the stables after all.

'Charming as usual...' a voice came from my right, and I turned to see Chloe arriving from the direction of the paddocks.

'I s'pose she's got her friends here too?' I asked.

'Yeah, Gemma and Kim are in the office.'

I glanced around. 'Where's Bev?'

Allie must seem like a giant to her.

'She's in Patch's stable keeping her head down.'

I let out a sigh. Hiding out might work for a while, but things were going to kick off eventually. 'Let's just keep an eye out for each other.'

I got Kyra out of her stable and took her down to the paddocks, and Chloe came along saying, 'I could do with checking on Eddie'.

I turned Kyra out into the paddocks as quick as I could so we could jog back up to the yard and Patch's stable.

'You okay in there?' I asked when we got there.

Bev looked up and smiled nervously. 'Gemma just told me Allie wants to see me in the office.'

'What for?'

'To check I know who my friends are.'

'What did you say?'

'That I'd go over when I was finished.'

'Really?'

'I've got to face her sometime.'

'We'll come with you,' asserted Chloe.

Bev made a not-sure face. 'I want to stand up for myself. You won't always be around to help.'

'But there's three of them...' I pointed out.

She nodded and a sudden shiver ran through her, showing how she really felt inside. 'Okay. Maybe if you could hang out somewhere nearby, so you can come if I call out?'

'How will we hear you?'

Bev concentrated briefly.

Can you hear this?

I jumped at the voice in my head. Chloe jumped next to me too.

'How'd you do that?' I gasped.

'One of the spells in that book.'

'But we gave it back to Jane.'

'I've read that book about a hundred times,' Bev said simply. 'And I've got a good memory.'

She looked fine as she came out of the stable, but when she went to lean her fork against the wall it rattled slightly as she let it go, like her hand was trembling.

'Better get it over with, I s'pose.'

She walked off towards the gap that led to the office.

Chloe stared after her. 'What happened to scared little Bev?'

'I think she's still scared.'

Bev glanced round and gave a small wave before she disappeared through the gap.

'Come on...' Chloe hissed. 'Let's get closer.'

She jogged over to the gap and I followed. From there we could see the menage gate, and the end wall of the office, and the start of the narrow path that led around the front corner of the office towards its door.

I beckoned Chloe to creep closer, and when we reached the end wall of the office, I pressed my ear against its rough splintery wood.

Nothing.

'What are you doing?' A snarl of a voice made me jump. Gemma! She'd just come around the corner in front of me.

'We're just going to the office.'

Kim appeared behind Gemma. 'You can't go in there.'

Then I heard someone cry out from the other side of the wall.

'Out of my way!' I went to barge past Gemma, but she grabbed my shoulders and slammed me against the wooden wall.

'You're not going anywhere,' she hissed in my face.

And then she was gone, knocked backwards so hard she slammed into Kim and they both fell down.

'Come on!' Chloe snapped and stepped past the sprawling limbs of the two girls.

I tried to follow but a hand grabbed my ankle. I twisted and kicked out blindly with my free foot.

'Owww!'

My ankle came free and I rushed after Chloe.

I saw her barge through the office door ahead of me. Three scrambling steps later I went through after her and slammed into her back. She was frozen just inside the office and staring like she didn't know what to do next.

What I saw took me a few moments to process.

Bev was sprawled on the sofa with her hand up to her nose and a bloody bogey stringing down between her fingers. And she was glaring intently at... my gaze swivelled to the right... Allie backed into the far corner of the office, looking terrified, and clutching her arm like it was hurting. And her eyes were fixed on something high up in the vaulted roof.

At first I couldn't see anything up there, but then a small flame jetted and I made out the shape of a tiny dragon squatting on a wooden beam.

'Call that thing off,' hissed Allie. 'Or you'll be sorry.'

'Get lost...' Bev mumbled.

Allie lashed out with a kick and caught Bev on the shin.

'Oww!'

The dragon leapt off its perch.

'No...!' Allie ducked down as tiny wings whirred over her head.

A bitter tang of burning hair caught in my nose, and Allie started batting at her head with both hands.

Then something crashed into my back and sent me and Chloe staggering towards the back wall.

Gemma and Kim again!

The little dragon went crazy.

It clattered around the office like a frenzied bronze bat, sending out puffs of flame and bashing into things.

Chloe dropped to the floor and pulled me down with her. Bev curled into a ball on the sofa and put her arms over her head.

Gemma and Kim screamed and bundled back out of the office as quickly as they'd come in. Allie ran after them, ducking down with her hands clamped over her head. She slammed the office door shut behind her and everything got quieter. The whirring of dragon wings quickly eased back to a steady buzz, then stopped completely. I looked up slowly. And saw the dragon sitting on the arm of the sofa with Bev stroking its head. She muttered some words to it and... pop... it disappeared.

Chloe and I pushed ourselves back up from the floor.

Bev had found a tissue from somewhere and was wiping her hands and nose.

'Are you okay?' I asked.

'Kind of... thanks for coming.'

Chloe snorted a short laugh. 'I don't think you needed us.'

'I was about to call for you. But then...' She waved the bloody tissue.

'She actually *hit* you?' I asked.

Bev nodded. 'She sent the others out. Then she started accusing me of making her fall off her horse. Then I said it served her right. And she lost it.'

'And you used that dragon spell on her?'

'Yeah, I had it ready in my head. And I'd practiced it loads, until I could make the dragons do what I want.'

'Was that why you were okay to come in here and face them?'

She shook her head. 'No, that was because of you two... I knew I wasn't on my own anymore.'

Chloe went over and pulled Bev up onto her feet, then we all gathered in for a group hug.

'Did the dragon burn her arm?' I asked when we'd broken apart again.

Bev nodded. 'Her hair too. D'you think she'll tell her mum and dad?'

An unexpected giggle bubbled out of me. 'What, that she got chased by a dragon?'

'They'd think she'd gone crazy,' agreed Chloe.

By the time we came back out of the office Allie, Gemma and Kim were gone.

Teagan and Megan said they'd seen them on their phones in the carpark, and that Allie's dad had come and picked them up.

Bev moaned that she'd have to look after Blake for another day.

'Why?' I asked. 'When Allie just hit you?'

'That's not Blake's fault,' she said simply.

She had a point... but then Blake was nearly as nasty as his owner.

For the rest of the day it stayed clear and sunny, but there was a chill in the air that made us all keep our fleeces on as we worked. It made me think about summer coming to an end and having to start at my new school. How was that going to work out, now we'd kind of declared war on Allie and all her friends?

Jane said she couldn't do our lessons that day because she was busy getting ready for tonight – whatever that meant. She told us to just ride our ponies in the menage to give them some exercise.

I took Kate out there with Bella just before lunchtime. Poor Kate seemed quiet and when I asked her what was wrong, she said it was because she'd seen Allie, Gemma and Kim in the carpark when they were leaving, and they'd looked really cross and said something horrible to her.

In the afternoon me and Chloe took Kyra and Eddie into the menage together; we set up a few small jumps and had fun taking turns going over them.

'I can't believe Eddie and Kyra get on so well,' Chloe said as we walked them around at the end to cool down.

The two ponies were happily walking next to each other with their ears pricked forwards.

I nodded but my mind was somewhere else. 'What d'you think Jane wants to do later?'

It seemed like this was the first time any of us had had the chance to talk about tonight without someone earwigging.

'Didn't she say she wanted to go to this Woolly Hole place?'

'Yeah. And to get there she needed our help.'

'D'you think she wants us to go with her?'

We decided we'd just have to wait to find out. It was nearly five o'clock already, so we weren't going to have to wait long.

People drifted off home, waving and saying 'bye', their horses put away in their stables for the night with new straw beds and water and hay.

Finally, only me and Chloe and Bev were left. We stood and chatted outside Patch's stable.

'D'you think we should go and knock on Jane's door?' Chloe wondered.

We hadn't seen Jane all day. It seemed strange, like she might've forgotten all about the sleepover and wanting our help.

'How could she have forgotten?' Bev asked. 'With all our bags piled up in her kitchen.'

'Good point,' agreed Chloe.

The sky above was clear, but was growing darker as the sun set. I checked my phone... 7.58pm. How had it got that late?

The sound of a door slamming shut made us all look up. It had come from the direction of Jane's house.

'D'you think that's her?' I breathed.

'Why're you whispering?' Choe murmured back.

'Don't know... why're you?'

That set us all off giggling.

Footsteps came stamping down the yard and we saw it was her, with her riding gear on and bundled up in a puffa jacket, and holding onto a bulging bin bag.

'I brought these for you,' she dumped the bag on the ground and started pulling out more puffa jackets. 'You might need them.'

They were all Jane-sized... which was okay for me... but a tight fit on Chloe, and way too big for Bev.

She left us trying jackets on and bustled over to Sade's stable.

We all glanced at each other.

'What's she doing?' Mouthed Chloe.

Bev and me shrugged.

A couple of minutes later she came back out leading Sade by her reins. The big horse was fully tacked up and ready to ride!

'Come on!' Jane said. 'Let's see how strong this magic is.'

She led Sade towards the menage and we all followed.

We watched as she opened the gate and went in, checked Sade's girth, then hauled herself up into the saddle.

It was getting dark properly now. There was a glow of orange in the sky beyond the paddocks, but the menage was pooled in shadow.

'Right!' Said Jane. Did she sound just a bit nervous? 'Just a warning, girls... this might be a bit of a shock... if it works.'

Jane set off around the edge of the menage, like a normal exercise session. She walked Sade up one side, then as she turned along the back she went into a trot, and then as she went by us again, she kicked Sade into a canter.

The big horse skipped around one full circuit of the menage, like it was no effort at all, and she could keep it up forever.

Then, as she reached the back fence for the third time, Jane pulled Sade into a tighter turn so she ended up cantering down the centre of the menage, heading straight towards us.

Jane was riding like there were jumps to go over... except all the jumps had been cleared away. When she reached about halfway down the menage, she leaned forwards over Sade's neck.

'What...?' I started to say.

Sade tucked in her forelegs and launched into the air with her powerful back legs.

Chloe muttered a word that would've got me into a lot of trouble if I'd said it at home.

Because Sade didn't come back down. She just kept going up, her legs cycling like she was cantering up a steep slope.

We turned, our necks craned back, and watched as the horse flew over our heads, a strange silhouette of horse belly and cantering hooves against the darkening sky.

'Oh... my... God!' Said Bev.

'You can say that again...' I muttered back.

'Hope Sade doesn't poo,' said Chloe.

Against the still-just-about-light sky it was easy to keep track of Jane and Sade. The dark shape of them kept going straight into the last orange glow of the sunset, getting smaller quickly, and when I thought they might just disappear over the tops of the trees that grew beyond the paddocks, they turned in a wide circle and came back towards us.

The shape of them gradually got bigger again. Then, all in a rush, they were back and flying so low over our heads that we all ducked, and Sade's hooves thudded and they were back in the menage. It was so dark now I could hardly see them, but I heard Sade canter away and then circle around and come back towards us again.

'Well, that worked... kind of...' Jane's words whooshed out as she brought Sade to a stop in front of us.

'You flew!' Gasped Bev, as Jane slipped her feet out of her stirrups and dropped down off Sade's back.

'Yes. We flew. We haven't done that for... a long time.'

'It was amazing,' said Chloe.

I nodded. 'Really sic.'

Jane laughed. 'That means good, right?'

'Yeah,' we all laughed.

Jane looked round at us all in the failing light.

'But I'm afraid it wasn't quite... sic... enough. Sade could fly when she was near you three, but we couldn't get much beyond the paddocks. So I'm afraid I was right, I am going to need your help.'

I waited for her to go on. The others kept quiet too.

Jane sighed. 'You're all going to have to fly to Woolly Hole with me.'

13

Flying Through the Night

'Oh my God... we're going to fly!' Chloe gasped as we got our ponies' saddles and reins from the tack room. Luckily there was a dim lightbulb in there so we could find our stuff.

I glanced at her and saw a mad grin that I knew must be mirrored on my face too.

Bev didn't look so keen, though. 'What if we fall off?'

I'd never fallen off Kyra yet, although I'd come close. But I was too excited to be scared.

'Ask Jane... see what she says,' I suggested as I hauled Kyra's tack out through the door into the gloom outside.

I stumbled down to Kyra's stable awkwardly holding my phone to use its flashlight. The pony snickered as she saw me coming. She sounded as excited as me.

It was super dark inside Kyra's stable and I leant my phone in the corner so I could see to get her saddle and bridle on. Then I led her outside and saw the bobbing white lights of Chloe and Bev's phones as they came across the yard with their ponies.

As we reached the menage there was a loud click and a buzz and the whole thing was suddenly bathed in stark yellow-white light. I glanced up and noticed for the first time there were floodlights set up on high poles at each corner of the menage.

The office door banged shut and Jane called out. 'We'll need the lights. For when we set off, and later when we get back.'

I was starting to get nervous now. My legs were shivery and weak, and there was a jitter making my tummy feel hollow.

'What happens if we fall off?' Bev asked Jane as soon as she joined us.

Jane smiled. 'I have something for that... gather around all of you.'

She got us to stand in a circle with her and hold hands. Then she muttered words that didn't sound like English under her breath. It was like a poem, with definite lines of speech, and with Jane's voice rising and falling like she was on the edge of singing. The jitters in my tummy eased and my legs firmed up. Then she spoke a final line louder than the rest, and a tingle fizzed into of my hands and on through every part of me.

'Oh!' Chloe muttered next to me and let go of my hand. And Bev did the same on the other side of me.

Jane nodded. 'Good. That was a soft-landing enchantment. If you fall off, it'll kick in before you hit the ground.'

I glanced at Chloe and Bev. That hadn't actually made me feel much better about the idea of falling off, and they didn't look too sure either. I decided I was going to hang on for dear life, whatever happened.

None of this seemed quite real. Had Jane really just flown up out of the menage, circled around in the sky and then landed back down here again? And could we do the same?

'Okay... no time to lose, does anyone need the loo?' Jane asked briskly.

Just mentioning it made me want to go, and from the sudden look on Chloe and Bev's faces it was the same for them.

Jane held our ponies while we ran up to the toilet in the carpark.

'Are we really doing this?' Chloe wondered as rushed back.

'I think so,' I puffed.

Jane handed out some small cans to us when we got back.

'I'm not allowed to have this,' Bev said unsurely.

The cans were energy drinks.

'We'll be travelling for most of the night... would you rather fall asleep when you're flying around up there?' Jane asked.

We all pulled the rings on top of the cans and glugged the contents down.

And then there was no delaying it anymore. We hauled ourselves up onto our ponies and in moments we were following Jane at a trot around the fence of the menage. It was weird with the floodlights on. It made everything outside the menage look black and impenetrable.

Jane kicked into a canter about halfway to the back fence, and ahead of me Chloe and Bev did the same. How had I ended up at the back? Kyra went into a canter without me asking.

Oh god!

Jane reached the back fence and turned in sharply like she had before and headed back down the centre of the menage.

'Just go into a jumping position!' Jane called out. 'And you'll be fine.'

Kyra followed Patch in a tight turn, and then we were all cantering down the centre of the menage.

'And jump!' Jane's voice drifted back to me, and I saw Sade leap into the air.

Eddie jumped next, and did exactly the same.

Next Patch climbed up into the air.

I was the only one left on the ground, but I could feel Kyra speeding up and gathering her legs under her. She was going to go, any moment! I just had time to stand up in my stirrups and lean forwards.

And... whoah. She jumped.

Jane had lied. It was nothing like going over a jump, more like being on a pony that was going really fast up a super steep hill. I felt my weight trying to drag me backwards and grabbed the front of the saddle.

Five scary cantering paces later I plunged into the blackness beyond the floodlights, but Kyra kept on climbing, higher and higher.

How could she see where she was going? I couldn't see a thing.

I just held on tight and my eyes slowly adjusted. Was that Patch's white rump ahead of me? And beyond him, a dark shape that might be Chloe and Eddie?

A road went by below, with streetlights dotted along each side and cars that looked weird from above; rectangular blocks of darker shadow with headlight beams lancing out in front.

We were still climbing. A chill shuddered through me and I was suddenly glad of the puffa jacket.

Everyone okay?

What? Was that Bev doing that speaking-in-your-head thing? But it didn't sound like her... it sounded like Jane.

I think so... came back, sounding majorly unsure. That was Bev.

Easy peasy! That sounded like Chloe.

Could I do it too? I tried speaking out loud, but kind of shouting in my head as well.

Are we going much higher?

Down below the road had merged into a bigger network of light-lined streets and highways. We had to be hundreds of metres up in the sky.

No, we can level off here.

And a moment later Kyra eased out of her climb and I didn't have to hold onto the front of the saddle anymore. I sat up straight as Kyra settled into an easy rolling gait.

Then pale light shimmered into existence as the moon came out from behind a cloud.

'Oh...' I muttered.

I could suddenly see Jane and Chloe and Bev ahead of me, and either side of their ponies a tracery of silver lines etched out the shape of long, graceful wings.

Just keep following me... it's rather a long way, I'm afraid.

None of us replied to Jane. What was there to say?

I settled into watching the world go by below.

In no time we were flying over London. I knew it was near because dad went there for work every day.

Some of the buildings soared up higher than we were flying, and Jane steered us around those.

What would anyone think, if they looked out of their office windows and saw four horses flying past? But then it had to be at least 10pm by now, so most people would've gone home. I had an urge to get my phone out and check the time, but the thought of dropping it stopped my hand reaching for my pocket.

London seemed to go on forever, the taller buildings giving way to squat black shapes, then to mazes of housing estates and high streets with lights from houses and shops glinting randomly, all connected by light-lined roads that circled and split and joined and split apart again in random patterns.

Then slowly the ground below turned into the dark of the countryside, cut through by single-stranded A-roads and dual-carriageway motorways, full of cars and lorries following their headlights to wherever they were going.

On and on we went. Kyra's rhythm was hypnotic. Rolling backwards and forwards, backwards and forwards. I would've dropped off to sleep for sure if it hadn't been for that energy drink... and the lurking terror of what it would be like to fall off Kyra into the darkness.

Hours and hours dragged by... or at least it felt like that... I had no way of telling how long we'd been flying.

Until finally...

We're nearly there, girls.

What? Jane's words had pulled me out of a daze.

Down below everything was black, so black it could have been an expanse of sea, or desert.

We'll soon be on the ground again. You've all done really well.

Really? I didn't feel that I'd done anything. Except for hold on and hope for the best.

Then Kyra's hooves clipped something. My head spun to look back and, in the pale moonlight, I could just make out the leaves and twigs of the top branches of a tree.

Kyra stretched and reached her front hooves out and I had to brace one hand on the saddle to stop from slipping forwards.

Thud... thud, thud, thud-thud, thud-thud.

Kyra cantered a few paces on firm ground before dropping to a walk.

We're down!

Dark shapes resolved in the silvery moonlight. A big horse and two ponies, which had to be Sade and Eddie and Patch. Kyra stopped and nosed the ground for grass to eat.

'Well done, everyone,' Jane's voice came out of the darkness. Her real voice, not the one in my head. 'We made it!'

How long had we been flying? I got my phone out.

02.12

More than four hours since we'd set off.

Small white lights flared, and I saw Chloe and Bev had their phones out again to use as flashlights. They jerked and weaved as the two girls dropped down onto the ground. Good idea! I was stiff and sore from being in the saddle for so long. I kicked my boots free of the stirrups, leaned forwards to swing my right leg over Kyra's back, then slid down onto the ground.

'All of you... slide those stirrups up on their straps... and twist and secure your reins. Then we'll leave the horses here untied, so they can come when we call them later.' Jane's voice seemed loud in the darkness and a part of me cringed. It felt like we should be whispering, that we shouldn't be here... wherever we were.

I did as Jane said, using my phone as a flashlight so I could see.

As I finished, I heard a small click and a yellow glow added to the stark white of our phones. I looked up and saw Jane was holding some kind of electric lantern.

'Come along, then,' she said and started walking away.

We all followed, me at the back again, the white light of my phone showing rough grassland under my feet.

A few minutes later we reached a wide gate in a fence with a stile next to it and a footpath sign. As we took turns to climb up and over the stile, I shone my phone on the sign.

Woolly Hole – ½ mile

It was pointing to the right down a narrow lane the other side of the stile.

Jane led the way along the lane, which felt like it was going slightly downhill. A half-moon looked down at us from the sky above, ghosting in between light clouds, and owls hooted from far-off trees.

It was really spooky.

The tiny lane met a bigger road and Jane turned left along it, and then no more than twenty paces further on she turned right into a big open space with a sign on a wooden post.

Woolly Hole – visitors parking

The space was empty. I imagined it in the daytime. Filled with cars with mums and dads and kids getting out and laughing or grumping about being dragged to see some stupid caves.

Jane stopped at a tall metal turnstile, which looked designed to stop anyone getting past it who wasn't allowed. She murmured a few words and there was a loud click, then she pushed the revolving gate and it let her through. We all pushed through the same as she had, the metal of the gate creaking in the quiet darkness, complaining at being used in the dead of the night.

'This way...' Jane was whispering at last, thank god.

Rough stone enclosed us, to either side and above. Mum and dad had taken us to some other caves once, up where we used to live, where you got taken by a guide around a load of tunnels and got to see stalag-tite-mite things and lit-up caverns and got to hear about how it was a total accident that the whole place got discovered at all.

Cold clammy cave smells crept into my nose as we went further and further in.

Jane seemed to know the way, and followed the twisty passages without hesitating. Finally, we ducked through an opening that had a sign above it.

No public access

And a few more turns later we got to a wide, open cavern.

I immediately got the whole *no public access* thing... in the middle of the cavern was a big hole, with nothing around it to stop anyone falling down. Jane's lamp showed jagged stone walls all around, and the high cavern roof above, but the hole itself was just a black maw that swallowed any light that went near it.

Chloe was giving me a what-the-hell-are-we-doing-here kind of look. I shrugged back. Bev was just staring around like she expected someone to jump out on her at any moment.

'Is this it?' I muttered a question, to everyone really, but it was Jane who answered.

'Yes, this is where the magic was drained away and sealed up.'

'So, what do we do now?' Chloe asked.

'We do a spell... something that should be impossible... like flying here should've been impossible.'

Jane sat down cross-legged and put her lamp on the ground next to her. 'Now, a little quiet for a moment, and then you might see... nothing... or, well, a kind of lightshow of magic either going into or coming out of the hole.'

She started muttering again, in that strange non-english language she'd used back at the stables for the soft-landing spell.

Bev leaned towards me and breathed close to my ear. 'That's Latin, I do it at school.'

Latin? Wasn't that some kind of old, dead language? It kind of made sense it might be used for ancient spells.

Jane's voice got louder like she'd got to the end of her spell, and then she went silent.

For a moment there was nothing.

Then lines of light began to spiral up out of the hole. Wibbling and wobbling like a tornado you see in the movies. At first, they were white and thin and hardly there at all, then thicker lines appeared, yellow, blue, green, red, and every other colour in between. They were silent, but in my head I imagined a swirling, roaring noise as light sucked up out of the hole.

Jane stared from where she sat, shaking her head in wonder, or maybe despair.

'The seal's broken,' she said. 'Why wouldn't they believe me?'

A hand tugged at the arm of my borrowed puffa jacket, and I looked down from the tornado of light to see Bev's frightened face. Colours flashed across her cheeks and glinted in her eyes.

'There's something wrong,' she whispered.

'Duh!' I murmured back, jerking my head at the light spiralling out of the hole.

'No...' She hissed. 'Something else.'

She pulled at my arm, and I saw she'd also grabbed Chloe's arm too.

There was something about the fear in her face... we let her pull us away from the hole, off to the side where there was a dark cleft in the cavern wall.

She didn't stop pulling until we were all hidden in the cleft.

I looked back. Jane was still sitting on the ground, unaware of us moving away. 'What about Jane?' I whispered urgently.

I went to run back to her but Bev grabbed my arm again. I tried to shake her off but Chloe grabbed me too. Even her eyes were wide with fear.

Then Bev closed her eyes and muttered words to herself, her voice rising and falling like Jane's did when she spoke the words of a spell.

Her eyes snapped open and bored into mine, no longer flickering orbs of reflected light, but dark pools made black by the shadows at the edge of the cavern.

Bev and Chloe kept a hold of me.

And yet...

I stumbled back out into the cavern and ran to Jane, leaning down like I was about to shake her shoulder.

'Stop!' A shouted command shook the still air of the cavern.

A tall figure dressed in a black cloak strode in from the passageway outside, followed by more figures, some smaller and some taller, but all dressed the same with hoods up over their heads.

14

Attack in the Dark

I looked up with shock on my face, and next to me Jane came out of her trance and pushed herself to her feet.

The tall figure, the one that had been the first to enter the cavern, raised her hand and pointed a thin-stick-thing at me and Jane. It was black, with a bright light pulsing at its end.

'Beatrice!' Jane exclaimed.

Beatrice... wasn't that Jane's sister's name?

'Jane...' Beatrice sighed. 'I had hoped you would not come here, like I'd hoped I was wrong about your abomination.'

Abomination? The woman... Beatrice... seemed to be glaring at me when she said that.

Jane was shaking her head. 'But you said you didn't believe the magic was coming back... and yet you have a wand?'

Beatrice flicked the wand and its tip made a glowing arc in the air, like a sparkler waved by a kid on bonfire night. 'This has nothing to do with the magic coming back, Jane... it's been charged from the Grand Coven's reservoir of magic.'

'Reservoir of magic?'

Whatever that was, Jane had obviously never heard of it.

Mutters of alarm and disapproval came from the group of figures behind Beatrice... like a secret had been told that shouldn't've been.

'For goodness' sake,' the tall figure glared round at the crowd. 'It doesn't matter who knows.' She turned back to Jane. 'When the magic was drained away, we kept some back... so the Grand Coven could still operate.'

The mutters came again, even louder, until Beatrice spun round and shouted. 'Enough!'

Everyone went quiet.

Beatrice turned back to Jane and me.

'So...' She waved her glowing wand towards the light spiralling out of the hole. 'The seal has been broken, and the magic is returning.'

'Yes,' replied Jane simply.

Beatrice waited, maybe for Jane to say more, but when she didn't Beatrice shook her head.

'I've been wondering why you brought your *concerns*...' She sneered that last word. '... to the Grand Coven. Was it to avert suspicion from yourself? Did you think that, by alerting us, we'd never imagine it was you who broke the seal in the first place?'

'Me?' Jane breathed.

'Let's be generous... maybe it was an unintended consequence... a side-effect of bringing your beloved sister, Cassiopeia, back into this world!'

Jane gasped. 'How would that even be possible?'

'You don't know? Really? That all you would need was a pool of magic, held back somehow, like the Grand Coven's reservoir... and some part of Cassiopeia's essence.'

'I don't have either of those things,' Jane said simply.

'And yet your stable is the place where a new coven has emerged, the first for over one hundred years? A pool of magic at work, I would say...'

Behind her there were new murmurings, agreeing with the point she'd just made.

'And,' she went on. 'As her sister, do you not have a lock of Cassiopeia's hair in your locket?'

'Aha' types of noises bounced around in the crowd of black cloaks behind Beatrice.

Beatrice's wand weaved in the air again and came to rest pointing at me.

'Then all you needed was a vessel. A new home for Cassiopeia's soul. So that she could be reborn into this world again.'

Me? Was she saying I was a vessel?

Jane looked round at me, shocked eyes denying what Beatrice had just said, about to say something reassuring. But then her look changed, and she murmured, 'Oh!' Like she'd just noticed something unexpected.

'But we are wise to your plan, sister. And we are here to cast Cassiopeia back into the hole again, before she regains her power,' Thundered Beatrice. 'And to seal her away again, along with her magic, forever!'

A crescendo of support came from the black-clothed mass behind Beatrice.

Beatrice's wand flared even brighter and zigzags of lightning lanced towards me, throwing me towards the hole.

I had no chance, the lightning kept battering me, until my boots slipped over the edge.

I fell into the tornado of light. But instead of disappearing into the depths of the earth, the flow of magic buoyed me up. To start with I hovered, struggling inside the streams of light, trying to claw my way back out.

Why didn't someone help me?

But Jane just watched sadly, and Chloe and Bev stayed hidden in their cleft at the side of the cavern.

The spinning light started to falter, no longer sucking up and out of the hole. What did that mean? Was the flow of magic changing? I started being pulled downwards and I reached out a desperate hand, hoping someone might grab it and save me at the last moment. But no one moved, and the last moment came and went, and I dropped out of sight. Lost forever to the world I knew, to my family, to my old friends and my new ones, and to whatever my future might've been.

The cavern was plunged into darkness.

'The magic seal is in place again!' Beatrice announced.

Her face looked manic, lit up by the glow at the end of her wand.

If this was her moment of triumph, it was spoiled by a bent old figure that barged out from the crowd behind her and cackled in her face. 'We need to leave now missy, if we want to get back before daybreak.'

'All right, all right,' Beatrice hissed back at her. 'We're finished here anyway, let's go.'

There was a lot of shuffling feet and mutterings and the black-cloaked figures turned around and left the cavern, not seeming to care who they'd left behind or what pain they'd caused.

Finally, the last one limped out of sight and Bev let out an exhausted gasp and collapsed onto the ground. Two things happened immediately after that; the tornado of light coming up out of the hole blazed back into existence, and I could suddenly see myself again.

I looked down at my arms, my legs, my boots. It had been weird, being invisible, like being a ghost.

Jane came over and bent down next to Bev. 'Are you all right, Beverley? You clever, clever girl.'

Bev managed to lift her head and nod. 'I think so... when I let go of the illusion my legs went all wobbly.'

Jane smiled. 'I don't know how you did it. Poppy looked so real. And then making everything go dark, like the magic had been sealed away again... that was genius.'

'I thought they wouldn't leave if the magic looked like it was still coming out.'

Then Jane came over to me, braced her hands on my shoulders and looked deep into my eyes. 'I promise you, Poppy, that everything Beatrice accused me with was wrong. I've never tried to bring back Cassiopeia, much as I loved her.' She heaved a disbelieving sigh. 'And I would never use another person the way she suggested, as a *vessel*, for another spirit to take over.'

'Was she lying, then?' I asked.

'I hope she was just mistaken... blinded by facts for which she could only see one conclusion.'

'My vote is that she was lying,' chipped in Chloe. 'She was awful.'

'I agree,' said Bev, who'd managed to sit up now.

Jane shrugged in the face of those strong opinions. 'We have a lot to work out, that's for certain. But we can't do it now. We need to get back. Just like them, we shouldn't be flying after daybreak.'

Jane rushed us out.

We ran through the passageways following Jane's bobbing yellow lantern, hoping we wouldn't bump into the back of the departing Grand Coven. But they must've been faster than they looked because we never saw them at all.

We reached the carpark outside and it was darker than when we went in. There was no moon anymore, even though the whole dome of the sky was ablaze with stars. Were we going to have to retrace our route down the lane and then along that footpath and up to the edge of the woods? That would take ages.

But Jane stopped and held up her lantern in the middle of the carpark and muttered a few words. What was she doing? And then I jumped out of my skin as hooves clattered on the tarmac and sent up sparks. Sade, Eddie, Patch and Kyra skidded and slipped to a stop and then trotted up to us.

'Come on, let's get going!' Hissed Jane, and we all fumbled to free up our reins and pull down our stirrups then haul ourselves up into our saddles.

'Everyone ready?'

We all shouted yes and Jane kicked Sade into a canter. Our ponies leapt away after the big horse, like they all knew we had to hurry.

In moments we were climbing into the dark envelope of the sky.

I had no idea how we stayed together as we rode back through the blackness, or how Sade up at the front knew which way to go. Maybe she was following the distant road lights below, no longer busy with cars and trucks at this dead hour of the morning. We kept going through the blackness for long hours, until a glow started to glimmer up ahead. We had to be heading east, I thought, if that was the glow of the sun starting to come up.

The light grew slowly, and soon I could make out the other ponies ahead of me, and Sade up at the front. It was a relief, but... hadn't Jane said something about us not being able to fly in daylight?

When it had been darker, we had sometimes flown over towns, and the splashes of light from streets and buildings so far below had made my toes tingle. But now, as the sky grew light, Jane seemed to be avoiding them.

How long would it be before we got back? Would we even make it before it became properly light? For now Jane kept galloping through the sky, and we kept following.

Something flittered in the air in front of me. A
small black shape. I caught a glimpse of a round face
and golden eyes.

Was that an owl?

Its eyes were wide and fearful. And staring right
at me.

It felt like a warning.

Then it twisted in the sky and swooped away. I
looked all around, but it was gone.

Something about it had seemed familiar. But
before I could pin that down...

Screech!

Another shape, much bigger, wheeled past me,
making me duck down in my saddle.

My head spun to watch it go past. It was as big as
Kyra and had wide black wings that were flapping
hard to turn it back around. Its head came into view,
jerking and searching until its eyes fastened on me,
then a mouth full of jumbled shards of teeth opened
and...

Screech!

Those wings dug hard into the air and the
monstrous shape came back again.

Gnarled, black claws reached out to grab me, but they closed on empty air as Kyra whinnied and shied away. I hit her neck hard and tried to hang on.

Screech!

Kyra dodged again and threw me backwards. And suddenly the world was turning over and over, and I couldn't feel the saddle underneath me anymore.

Wind whistled past my ears as I plummeted down through the early morning gloom.

I tumbled and spun downwards, downwards... towards the still-dark land below. I scrunched into a ball and waited to hit the ground, counting the seconds in my head... how many more did I have?

Then a huge hand, or a sudden updraft of air, or something between the two, caught me and the whistling in my ears dropped away to nothing, and I sensed I was falling more slowly until... leaves swooshed and branches snagged at my puffa jacket... then, Ouch... my shoulder hit something hard that bounced me sideways... and, Ooof... I slammed down onto soft, musty ground.

I rolled onto my left side and gasped ragged breaths, getting used to the fact I was still alive and somehow back down on the ground.

An image of Jane muttering words, and all of us holding hands, swam into my head. The soft-landing spell!

'Call that a soft landing?' I muttered.

Then clattering, swooshing noises, like something else falling through the treetops, shattered the morning stillness, followed by a thud that made the ground tremble.

Had that monster followed me down?

I rolled and got onto my feet. Everything hurt.

I could just about make out tree trunks all around me. I didn't dare move in case my feet rustled the dry leaves and gave me away.

Then something landed in front of me with a flutter of almost-silent wings.

That owl!

It stared at me with those familiar eyes for a moment, then its head swivelled as a noise sounded up from somewhere out under the trees.

Thud... drag. Thud... drag. Thud... drag.

Something big was hauling itself across the leafy ground, coming closer and closer.

The owl looked back my way once more, then leapt up into the sky.

Thud... drag. Thud... drag. Thud... drag.

And then the monster was there, between two large trees, looming over me. Its leathery wings were folded on its back like hunched shoulders, and its talons scrunched up the ground as it stared at me.

Then its horrible mouth opened... **Screech!** And a warm stench washed across me, clogging in my nose and throat.

The monster leapt high and came at me talons-first, like it wanted to grab me and launch back up into the sky.

I fell backwards.

I should've rolled sideways and ran away through the trees. Or grabbed a branch and tried to fight the thing off. But all I did was fall backwards.

The talons closed in on me...

Screech!

Then... slam! The black thing was gone.

What?

Had I seen a white shape smash into it?

A horrible smell swamped the early morning air, sharp and metallic and sick-making.

Then hooves clopped on the woodland floor and a something big came back out from between the trees.

It was a horse... no, it was a unicorn.

The muscled animal was way bigger than Kyra, bigger even than Sade, and when it ducked its head towards me, I saw its horn was long and sharp and coated in redness with ragged lumps of black flesh still clinging to it.

It lifted its head to the sky and whinnied. And from somewhere up above I heard an answering call. I glanced up... was that Kyra? And when I looked back down again the unicorn was gone and instead the owl was sitting on the dried-leaf ground and peering up at me. It hooted once and flew away.

Kyra found me first, her hooves swishing the piles of dead leaves as she came out from under the trees. She whinnied loud and in seconds the others appeared from different directions, Sade with Jane, Eddie with Chloe and Bev with Patch.

'Poppy, are you okay?' Chloe jumped down and hauled me onto my feet.

'What's that smell?' Bev asked with a screwed-up nose.

Jane brought Sade up close. 'Let's talk later, girls. If we get going quickly we might still make it back.'

I wasn't sure I wanted to fly again, but it wasn't like I had any choice. Jane and Sade led us away through the trees and it wasn't long before we reached a clearing that was big enough for her to kick Sade into a canter and launch into the air. We all followed, although Jane insisted I went right behind her this time, with Bev next and then Chloe at the back.

It was much lighter now, although still very early in the morning. There wouldn't be too many people up and about to see us... and if they did, would they believe their eyes anyway?

Finally, we started dropping downwards and up ahead I saw a lit-up rectangle on the ground. The menage at Windwicche stables!

We cantered out of the sky like we were riding downhill, and all came to a soft landing on the sandy soil of the menage. I slid down off Kyra's back and was never so grateful as when my feet hit firm ground again.

15

My Familiar

'Poppy... wake up!' Someone was digging me in the ribs.

I opened my eyes. The ceiling above me wasn't right. It was smooth and painted creamy white, not uneven and patchy and flaking. Where was I? And why hadn't mum got me up yet? From the amount of light in my room, it had to be late.

'Come on, Jane's made us breakfast.'

Wait... was that Chloe? I twisted around and saw her standing looking down at me.

Everything came back in a rush; the night ride through the sky, the spooky caves, the terror of falling off Kyra, and that black thing trying to grab me. I sat up quickly. I was on a sofa with blankets on top and under me, still dressed in the same clothes as last night.

I was in Jane's snug.

Chloe was giving me a look. 'You gotta get up, it's after ten o'clock.'

'Okay.'

I pulled myself up and followed her into the kitchen.

'Poppy!' Jane saw me and rushed over. 'How are you feeling?'

She hugged me and I mumbled that I was fine.

Jane stood back and gave me a disbelieving look. 'Tired, traumatised, scared to death... those I'd believe, but *fine*?'

I shrugged. 'Maybe *numb's* a better word?'

Jane squeezed my shoulders and led me to the breakfast bar.

There was juice and tea and waffles and berries and maple syrup. Bev was already there tucking in and looked up to give me a muffled 'Hello'. Once I was sat down Chloe took the stool next to me.

I glugged down a glassful of juice... God, I was thirsty.

Jane nodded in approval. 'Eat up, Poppy. And the rest of you. Then we need to talk.'

While we ate, she disappeared into the snug and came out again with an armful of blankets, taking them away into another part of the house.

Memories from last night skulked around inside my head, but I tried to ignore them and think about something else.

It didn't help that Chloe and Bev kept asking questions. Like 'How come you fell off Kyra?' And 'D'you think you really are Cassiopeia?' And 'What'll the Grand Coven do when they work out we tricked them?'

I kept my focus on breakfast. Sipping more juice, pouring maple syrup, cutting up waffles and taking big mouthfuls.

'I just dunno...' I stuttered finally, when both of them stopped talking and seemed to be waiting for me to say something.

Jane bustled back at that point. 'Come on everyone!'

She got us back into the snug and sat us down on the sofa, then she flopped down into the armchair opposite. 'What a night!'

And suddenly I couldn't ignore the memories anymore. Especially one massive one...

'Why did they want to throw me down that hole?' I asked. It came out trembly and scared and I felt prickling in both of my eyes.

Jane gazed at me. 'They think Cassiopeia is inside you – reborn into this world.'

I remembered all those accusing, hating, eyes, staring at me... well, at Bev's illusion of me... while that awful Beatrice blasted me into that hole with her magic wand. And all because...

'But I'm not, am I? I'm not Cassiopeia?'

Jane shrugged. 'I'm not sure.'

'But... wouldn't I know?'

'Maybe not. If her spirit was inside you, it would take time to grow, it wouldn't take over right away.'

Not reassuring. Not reassuring at all.

'What makes them think I'm her, anyway?'

'Because of Kyra.'

'Kyra? What does she have to do with this?'

'Kyra was Cassiopeia's pony. And she's never let anyone else ride her... until you.'

Oh.

'But that doesn't make me her, does it? Not for sure?'

'No,' Jane agreed. 'Not for sure.' But I could see the uncertainty in her eyes.

Another memory pounced on me... the second most massive one. 'And what was that black monster-thing when we were flying back?'

Everyone looked confused.

'What black monster-thing?' Asked Bev.

'The black monster-thing that attacked me and knocked me off Kyra.'

'We thought you, like, just fell asleep or something,' said Chloe.

'Thanks.'

'What did it look like?' Asked Jane.

'It was big. The size of a horse at least. With huge, kind of, bat wings. And teeth... it had a lot of teeth... and horrible talons that it tried to grab me with.'

Jane looked confused. Like she was trying to remember something but couldn't quite do it.

'Are you sure?' She asked.

I nodded. 'Your spell soft-landed me down in those woods. But then the black thing followed me down there and tried to grab me again.'

'But,' Jane was staring at me like I was crazy. 'How come you're... still okay?'

'I wouldn't have been. But then a massive unicorn appeared out of nowhere and, I don't know, got rid of it.'

Jane opened her mouth, shut it, then opened it again. 'A unicorn?'

I nodded.

'Lucifer...' she breathed.

And at that moment, I felt a soft brush against my ankles.

'Meow'.

And something black jumped up onto my lap.

It was Seefa!

Jane stared at Seefa like she'd seen a ghost.

'How did you get here?' I asked the cat.

Last time I'd seen her was... back at home when I'd left for the stables yesterday morning. I tickled her ears and she curled into a ball on my lap.

I looked up at the others. 'D'you think she could've sneaked into mum's car yesterday and jumped out when we got here?'

Jane shook her head slowly. 'She wouldn't have had to do that... when did you get her?'

'Not long after I started at the stables. Mum said she just turned up outside our back door one day.'

'And... you never saw her here before then, at the stables?'

I shook my head. 'No.'

'Not even... in the feed store, or near it?'

The feed store? Why had she mentioned the feed store?

'No… I saw something else in the feed store, but not Seefa.'

'What exactly?'

I hesitated. It still seemed wacky talking about what I'd seen. Even after all the other weird stuff that'd happened since.

'Kind of a… little person.'

'Oh, my Lord.' Jane sounded like something devastating had happened.

'What?'

'That's Lucifer.'

'Lucifer?'

Bev cut in. 'Isn't that the devil?'

Jane shook her head, still staring at my cat. 'Before that… it was the name for Venus… the morning star.'

What did any of that matter? 'This is just my cat, Seefa.'

'Lucifer… Seefa… is a pixie, Poppy. She can take different forms; a small person, a black cat, an owl… and her most fearsome form, a white unicorn.'

Everything fell into place. I hadn't seen that little person since Seefa had come to live in our house. And there'd been an owl last night, trying to warn me. And a unicorn had saved me.

283

'It looks like she's your familiar now,' Jane went on. 'Which is worrying.'

'What's a familiar? And why is it worrying?'

'A familiar is a wicche's companion. And it's worrying because... Lucifer was Cassiopeia's familiar.'

Everyone went quiet while they thought about that. Even I started to believe it about Cassiopeia's spirit. It made a fluttery feeling shiver down my back.

Bev broke the silence. 'Isn't there some way to find out for sure... you know... if Cassiopeia's...'

I finished the question for her. 'Somewhere inside me?'

'I don't know of any,' Jane replied.

'But we can't just let her take Poppy over,' groaned Chloe.

I let them go on talking about me like I wasn't there, treating me like I was suddenly this huge problem, while I zoned out and tried to poke and pry around inside my head. If another spirit was in there, wouldn't I be able to get a glimpse of it, somehow feel its presence?

But there was nothing. I just felt like me, same as I'd always felt.

Bev said something that made me tune in again.

'Didn't Beatrice say you had a lock of Cassiopeia's hair? Couldn't we use that somehow?'

Jane reached behind her neck and unclasped her locket chain. We all leaned forwards as she carefully clicked open the front. Inside was a curl of yellow hair tied around the middle with thin cotton. 'This is her's.'

I found myself reaching to touch it. I half expected Jane to pull it away, but she let me go ahead and stroke a finger along its length.

'Do you feel anything?' She asked.

I shook my head. 'Should I?'

'If you were her, maybe. But I don't know.'

'Could we use that?' Bev asked.

Jane shook her head. 'I should know... but, things are not as clear to me as they once were.' She sighed in frustration. 'Maybe I'm getting old.'

I didn't dare ask how old she was, I wasn't sure I wanted to know. It was starting to seem like wicches could live a very long time.

'Are there any spell books?' Asked Bev. 'More serious ones, that I could look through to see if there's something we could try?'

Jane put one palm to her forehead, like she'd forgotten something really obvious. 'Yes... of course there are.'

She clicked the locket shut and pulled herself up out of her armchair. 'Follow me.'

She took us out through the kitchen and then to a door at the other end that led into a wide hallway, where she stopped in the middle and pulled a floor-rug to one side. Set into the wooden boards underneath was a large square trapdoor. She grabbed an iron ring and hauled the trapdoor open, and we saw wooden steps leading down into the dark.

Jane went down them first and we all followed, until we all stood on a stone basement floor. Tall shapes hulked around us in the gloom of the windowless space and the air smelled like musty paper.

'Fiat lux...' Jane muttered, and seemed as surprised as we were when the basement was suddenly flooded with light.

Around us, tall bookcases marched away in every direction, with gaps between them just big enough for a person to squeeze down.

'This way...' she said, heading off down one of the gaps. '... I think.'

286

It was like a maze once we started down the gaps. There were corners and T-junctions and dead-ends, and the whole time the spines of books peered at us as we went by. There were fat books and thin books, and old books and newer books, there were even whole racks of what looked like magazines.

Whenever I had the time to decipher a title on one of the books, it was clearly magical. There must've been thousands of them on these shelves. How could there be so many books about magic? How could anyone ever read them all?

Chloe was dragging along looking bored after five minutes, I made it to ten minutes, but a half hour later Bev was still wide awake, her eyes sparkling and alive, goggling at the shelves like she wanted to stop and read every book.

Jane finally paused after forty minutes. 'Maybe here...' She said with uncertainty prickling at the edges of her voice.

Bev took over and started searching the titles methodically.

'There!' She said quietly and pointed. 'Chloe, can you reach it?'

Chloe jumped like she'd just woken up from a doze. 'Where?'

287

Bev was pointing at the top shelf. 'Fifth book along.'

Chloe reached up and slid the book out, then handed it to Bev. I peered over her shoulder. On the cover it said...

Sisterhood tokens – power and peril

Bev leafed through the book, flicking dust up into the air that tickled my nose, and after a few moments she said, 'Yes, can I take this one upstairs?'

We left Bev in the snug and promised we'd look after Patch and Blake, so she could focus on finding a spell to work out if Cassiopeia was inside me. And to get rid of her, I hoped.

I didn't want to think about it, but I couldn't stop.

Suppose her spirit was inside me, in my head or whatever, would it be the end of me if she took over? And would that happen gradually, or suddenly with no warning?

I kept telling myself it was all rubbish, that I'd *know* if she was really in there.

But... why had Kyra chosen me? And Seefa as well? Had they sensed Cassiopeia's presence somehow? Maybe they already knew she was there. I nearly asked Kyra straight out when I was leading her down to the paddocks, but I was too scared of what her answer might be.

That day passed by like everything was normal. So normal it kind of freaked me out. Everyone kept doing what they usually did, looking after their horses, mucking out, cleaning tack, and chatting about stuff. Allie and her friends, once again, didn't turn up, and so everyone was a lot more relaxed.

I got the chills a couple of times as I worked, usually when I was on my own, when the memory of the hole in the cave, or the black thing trying to grab me, caught me off guard.

I wondered if that black thing was dead. Seefa must've skewered it with her unicorn horn. Could it have survived that?

In the middle of the afternoon Bev came and found me. She was carrying the spell book under one arm.

'Hi Poppy, d'you know where Chloe is?'

It turned out Chloe was down at the paddocks leaning on the front fence and staring at nothing. When we saw her, we went over and leaned on the fence either side.

'Oh my god,' she gasped. 'You made me jump.'

'Sorry,' Bev said. 'But we all need to talk.'

'Have you found the spell?' Chloe asked.

Bev sighed. 'No, not yet.'

Relief washed through me. Was I really that scared of finding out for sure if there was someone else inside me?

'But this book got me thinking about something else,' she went on.

'What?' I asked, braver now I knew it wasn't going to be about me.

'All this sisterhood stuff... and how it works.'

She told us how wicches in a coven sometimes shared locks of hair, and that it was a big trust thing because it gave them power over each other.

'How?' Asked Chloe.

'If a wicche has some of your hair, or even your nail clippings or whatever, she can cast spells on you from a distance.'

'Okay... interesting... but why does that matter?'

'Well... I asked Jane, since they were sisters and all that, whether she also had a lock of Beatrice's hair.'

'And did she?'

Bev nodded. 'She did. In the other side of her locket. But she had to open it to check. Like she wasn't really sure.'

Me and Chloe must've looked blank because she gave us a *duh* look. 'Don't you get it? If Jane has a lock of Beatrice's hair, then Beatrice must have a lock of Jane's hair too.'

'And, so what?' Asked Chloe.

'Well, I think that Beatrice might've used it to put a spell on Jane.'

I still wasn't getting this.

'What sort of spell?' I asked.

'One that's... clouding her mind or something... making her get confused.'

Had I ever noticed Jane getting confused? Not about normal things, like riding, or looking after horses...

But maybe about magical stuff? 'I suppose she didn't sense that there was magic here, not until we showed her that spell working.'

'And she never noticed Bella was being spooked using magic, even though it was right under her nose,' Chloe added.

Bev suddenly turned away blinking.

Way to go Chloe!

I reached out and squeezed Bev's arm. 'It wasn't your fault, Bev.'

Chloe moved up close to Bev and hugged a big arm round her shoulders. 'Allie made you do it.'

'Anyway,' Bev managed after a few moments. 'If Jane is under a spell, we need to break it... and I think I've found a way.'

Bev turned back to the fence and rested her book on it, then opened it at a page near the end. The heading at the top of that page said...

Breaking of bonds

Under the heading there was a whole load of writing, along with a list of ingredients and a hand-drawn picture of a small bowl over a fire.

'Looks complicated,' Chloe said.

'Can you do it?' I asked.

Bev nodded. 'I think so... but there's one big problem. Jane's not gonna agree to it.'

'Why not?' Chloe and I asked together, then shared a quick smile.

'Breaking a sisterhood bond is kind of a big thing... and if Beatrice really does have her under a spell, I bet part of that would be to keep the bond intact whatever happens.'

'So, does that mean we can't try it?' I asked.

'No, it means we'll have to trick her into it.'

16

Breaking the Spell

We sent Bev back to work on the spell. We'd all
agreed that we should do it today, if we were going to
do it at all. Who knew what Beatrice and her Grand
Coven might do once they worked out they'd been
tricked.

'She's clever, isn't she,' Chloe said to me as we
brought Kyra, Eddie and Patch up from the paddocks
for the night.

'You mean Bev? Yeah, way cleverer than me,' I
agreed.

'Or me,' muttered Chloe. 'But d'you think she's
right?'

Good question. I'd been worrying about it ever
since we'd sent her off to work on the spell. 'I hope
she is.'

'Me too... 'cos Jane's going to go ballistic.'

Bev was waiting for us when we got back up to the
stables. 'It's ready. We're gonna meet Jane up at her
house at five.'

That meant we had to rush. We only just
managed to get the ponies settled in their stables and
up to Jane's house in time.

When we got there, Jane waved us inside and took us straight down to the cellar. 'Bev's been working very hard,' she said as we reached the bottom of the steps. 'So we should soon know for sure if Cassiopeia's spirit is inside you, Poppy.'

She glanced at me and I felt instantly guilty. But if it showed in my face, she mistook it for fear because she suddenly gave me a hug. 'Don't worry... I promise we'll find a way to make things right.'

She led us to a space away from all the bookshelves where Bev was sitting at a round table. In the middle was a metal plate and on top of that was a small pot. Bev was stirring the pot's contents with what looked like a thin branch off a tree.

'Come on,' Jane said with hushed excitement. 'Sit down.'

There were enough chairs around the table for all of us.

I tried to catch Bev's eye as I sat down, but she kept focused on the pot and her stirring. I realised she was muttering low words under her breath, that rose and fell like a poem, but which I couldn't quite make out.

We all watched her for about a minute, then suddenly she looked up and around and her gaze settled on Jane. 'Do you have the locket?'

Jane took it off from around her neck and went to click the front of it open.

'No!' Bev commanded. 'It must be me who opens it.'

A cloud of confusion passed across Jane's face but was gone as soon as it came. 'I seem to have forgotten so much,' she muttered as she handed the locket to Bev.

Bev put her stick down and took the locket, then dangled it by its chain over the steaming pot as she uttered some final words.

Then she stopped, and the silence was like at a church service between hymns. It went on and on until I started getting an urge to cough.

'Now!' Bev said suddenly.

And she brought the locket away from the pot and levered it open with her fingers. Then in one quick movement she took out a lock of brown hair and reached back towards the pot.

'No that's Beatrice's...' started Jane, lunging forwards to grab Bev's hand.

But Bev was too quick... the lock of hair dropped into the pot.

What happened next was like a silent explosion. My ears went hollow as a blast of air hit me in the face. I got the sense that the blast kept going past me, through the bookshelves and the walls and the floor and the ceiling, then out, further, down through the earth, up into the sky, and out along the ground, an expanding sphere that would go on forever.

Jane stood frozen, half out of her seat, her hand reached towards Bev's, her face twisted in rage.

What would she do next? Start yelling at us? Throw us out of her house?

But what she actually did was collapse, suddenly and completely, like a puppet with its strings cut.

Her head hit the table with a crack that made me wince. The pot got knocked sideways and skittered away on the floor – weirdly not spilling a load of liquid – but just sending a waft of smoke away under the bookcases. Then Jane kind of rolled and slumped off the table, right into Chloe's lap.

Chloe grabbed her around the waist to stop her falling any further, and I reached to cradle her head in my arms so it didn't hit anything else.

Then I looked up and found we were all staring at each other.

What had we just done?

We all, well mostly Chloe, hauled Jane's limp body back up the cellar steps and into the snug, where we settled her down on the sofa.

I glanced a question at Bev. 'Is she going to be okay?'

I could tell that Bev didn't know. 'I just did the spell... it didn't say what would happen afterwards.'

Jane groaned and we all looked down at her.

Her eyes opened and twitched around, taking in the walls of the snug, the sofa she was laying on, and all of us watching her.

'Oh, my Lord,' she whispered. But not in an accusing way. More in a totally-amazed way. 'How long have I been sleeping?'

We glanced at each other. It was a strange question.

I shrugged. 'About... five minutes.'

Jane swung her legs down and sat up straight. 'Then... when did all this happen?'

'All what?' Bev asked.

'The magic...' Jane wobbled up onto her feet. 'You girls...' She managed to get to the window and levered it open and peered out. 'Everything...'

None of us had a clue what she was going on about.

She turned back around and fixed her eyes on Bev. 'You broke my sisterhood bond with Beatrice.'

Bev nodded but didn't say anything, she looked petrified.

'That was very brave,' Jane moved her eyes to take in Chloe and me as well. 'I can see now... everything there is to see.'

She opened her arms to us for a group hug, and then she pulled us together tightly. 'We're all in terrible danger.'

Terrible danger?

Would that be more danger than last night when I was nearly killed twice? Actually, three times, if you counted falling off Kyra from way up in the night sky.

I pulled out of our hug. 'What danger?'

Jane made us sit down on the sofa before she explained.

'Everything's getting clearer. Something's been muddying my mind... stopping me seeing what's going on around me. Especially anything to do with magic or Cassiopeia.'

Cassiopeia? Did that mean Jane knew if her spirit was inside me now? I didn't want to ask... but then... maybe I did.

Jane focused on me. 'No, Poppy... I still can't see if she's inside you.'

Then she glanced around the walls of the snug like she could see beyond them.

'But I can feel her presence,' she muttered. 'She is here somewhere.'

'So...' Chloe prompted. 'What about this we're-all-in-terrible-danger thing?'

'Yes. Sorry. Beatrice... my sister... will soon realise we tricked her. And then she'll come for Poppy again.'

Something about all this didn't add up.

'But how come I got attacked on the way back last night? Surely, that means she's worked it out already.'

Jane turned and held my gaze for long seconds, then...

'Rattarak!' She gasped.

'What?'

'The creature that attacked you last night. It sounds like Rattarak.'

'What's Rattarak?'

'Beatrice's familiar. A pixie, like Lucifer. His flying form is a giant bat.'

Chloe made a strangled noise. 'Look Jane, I know she's your sister and all that, but that Beatrice is a complete troll!'

Jane nodded. 'If that means bad, you might be right.'

Different expressions fleeted across Jane's face, like she was rewinding things in her head, catching up with things that'd happened and seeing them properly for the first time.

'You said Rattarak was trying to grab you?' She checked with me.

I nodded.

'Maybe Beatrice sent him to capture you, rather than hurt you.'

Whatever that thing had been trying to do, it had been horrible and scary.

'And if that's the case, she'll try to get you again,' Jane went on. 'And then, I suppose, go back to Woolly Hole and finish the job of banishing... Cassiopeia.'

By Cassiopeia, Jane meant me.

'I think I just want to go home,' I muttered.

I didn't like our rented house, and my temporary bedroom, but that suddenly seemed like the comfiest, safest place to be in the world. Where everything was boring and nothing weird ever happened.

Jane hugged me. 'She'd find you there. And then your family would be in danger too.'

In that case, what choice did I have? I'd just have to stay at the stables until whatever was going to happen... happened.

'Hi Mum!' I chirped into my mobile, trying to sound like there was no terrible danger going on anywhere and everything was fine.

'I was just about to come and get you,' mum's voice came back.

'That's what I'm calling about... would it be okay if I stayed another night here?'

'I just made your tea, Poppy.'

'Please... Chloe and Bev and staying too.'

Mum didn't take much persuading; she actually sounded pretty smug that her stables idea had worked out so well.

Chloe and Bev didn't have any trouble with their parents either... anyone would think they didn't want their teenage daughters back home just yet.

After that Jane got us to prepare. She told us to tack up our ponies and leave them in their stables, ready for a quick escape if we needed it. Then she got us to practice holding hands in a circle with her to share our magic. She said she knew a lifetime's worth of spells, but we had the raw magic of youth, and so working together would give us our best chance.

Jane got me to ask Seefa to fly out in her owl-form to patrol the skies, so we'd know if anyone was approaching by air, and she said she'd already set up alarm-spells on the ground, to warn us of anyone coming towards the stables on foot.

Then all we could do was sit in Jane's snug and wait.

Bev spent the evening reading another spell book, which had on its cover...

Offensive Spells

I sat next to her and stared into space, my mind hopping through everything that had happened over the last six weeks.

Chloe snuggled into the corner of the sofa and dropped off to sleep after ten minutes. How did she do that?

And Jane was in her armchair, and then she wasn't, and then she was again. She was jittery. Up one moment pacing the room. The next sitting back down and giving big sighs. Then up and pacing again.

Late evening turned into night, then into early morning, which then dragged by with us all dropping into and out of dozes until the first fingers of dawn started to lighten the sky outside.

And nothing happened. No tripping of alarms, no alerts from Seefa... nothing.

'I don't understand,' muttered Jane as the hands of the clock over her fireplace clicked onto seven o'clock in the morning. 'If they were coming, they would've flown here in the dark and arrived long ago.'

She pushed herself up from her armchair for about the hundredth time. 'Maybe they'll come tonight instead.'

Which wasn't good. We couldn't just keep waiting here every night for them to turn up. Sooner or later mum would put her foot down and say I had to come home. And then what would happen?

Jane disappeared into the kitchen and soon delicious smells of waffles and hot chocolate got us up on our feet and heading through to get breakfast.

By seven-thirty I was finished and sitting watching Chloe demolish yet another waffle. Bev had already disappeared back into the snug to keep reading, and Jane was putting plates in the dishwasher.

'Is it okay to go down to the yard?' I asked.

I felt like some fresh air – and I wanted to see Kyra.

Jane nodded and waved me away. 'Yes, go... you can get Kyra untacked.'

As I walked away down Jane's path outside, I couldn't help checking the sky. It was a late summer blue, marred only by a few wispy streamers of clouds, and way up high by a trail from a jet plane, already smudged and dispersing.

A couple of cars were in the car park, and probably other cars had already dropped people off. I'd never been here this early before and didn't know how busy it got. I headed straight down through the yard to Kyra's stable.

The beautiful golden pony had her head hanging over of the top of her stable door and watched me as I got closer.

'I bet you want to get that saddle and everything off.'

I got the impression that she agreed, but no words sounded in my head.

I opened bottom door and reached to take off her bridle. Then I stopped.

'What about a run round the menage?' I was asking myself as much as I was asking her.

Kyra snickered enthusiastically.

'Okay then...' I led her out of the stable and she skittered along beside me, full of energy.

'Easy!' I laughed.

In the sunshine and with other people bustling around the yard, all the drama of our long night of waiting seemed a million miles away.

The menage was empty and all the jumps and poles were stacked along the sides. I opened the gate and led Kyra in, then closed it behind us. Then I pulled her stirrup leathers down and untwisted her reins and hauled myself up onto her back.

It felt great.

We walked around the menage once, then trotted another circuit, but I could feel Kyra wanted to go faster so I kicked her into a canter. We did three more full circuits before something made me glance upwards.

Oh my god!

The morning sky was filled with the dark shapes of flying horses.

17

Cassiopeia's Return

Hooves thudded down everywhere into the sandy surface of the menage.

Kyra circled and reared, spooked by so many heavy horses landing all around her. I patted her neck to calm her... sensing she might panic and bolt any moment.

'Stay right there!' A loud voice commanded, and I looked up and saw Beatrice between me and the menage gate. She was riding a beautiful black stallion and holding her wand ready above her head.

I felt Kyra gather her legs under her and I hauled at her reins. 'No!'

Lines of lightning lanced out towards us and sent a fountain of sand up in front of Kyra. She stumbled backwards and I felt myself falling.

There was no way I was going to stay on. I curled into a ball and waited to hit the ground.

Everything went into slow motion. Shouts around me stretched out weird and elongated. Then the ground crunched into my shoulder and threw me into a roll.

I sat up and watched Kyra go mad, bucking and running at the horses surrounding us. They backed away, jostling each other, giving the pony more and more space, until suddenly she twisted and leapt into the air. She flew up and away over their heads, climbing into the sky at a flat-out gallop.

And then I was on my own.

There had to be twenty horses in the menage, surrounding the open area that Kyra had cleared with her crazy running around. They skittered and wheeled about but didn't come any closer.

'Cassiopeia!' That was Beatrice's voice again, loud and shouting in my direction.

'I'm not Cassiopeia, I'm Poppy!' I shouted back, but even to me it sounded silly. If only I had a more dramatic name.

Beatrice just sneered and turned her horse away.

'Make a path!' She yelled, waving at the horses in the menage to move to the sides.

Then I saw something huge coming down out of the sky, right towards me! I scrambled and rolled away just in time, then twisted back to stare behind me as a whole team of horses' hooves thumped down, followed by the heavy wheels of a wagon that crashed and bounced and made the ground shake.

A huge ugly creature sat in the driving seat of the wagon, wearing tattered clothes that did nothing to hide the massive, knotted muscles in its arms. It hauled on a brake lever at its side and the wagon slewed around to a stop in front of the menage gate.

Something dropped inside me. Built onto the back of the wagon was a cage with dull metal bars. Was that for me?

'What are you waiting for!' Beatrice yelled out. 'Throw her inside!'

Figures in black robes dropped down off their horses and stalked towards me. Coming closer and closer.

Then an owl flapped down and landed in front of me.

'Seefa!'

The owl turned its head to gaze at me... then it hopped up into the air and...

Hurromph!

... its shape stretched and morphed into something huge and white. The unicorn from the woods.

The great white beast pawed the ground and lowered its head, twisting and turning to threaten the wicches around me with its sharp horn.

They started backing away again. Yes!

'It's just a Pixie!' Beatrice screeched. And more lightning flashed from her wand and seared across the unicorn's breast, making it stagger back a few paces before standing firm and pawing the ground again.

One by one of the wicches around me pulled out their own wands from inside their robes.

No! They were going to hurt Seefa!

Thud... thud, thud.

What?

Kyra had landed back in the menage, right next to Seefa.

Then...

Thud... thud, thud. Thud... thud, thud. Thud... thud, thud.

Sade, Eddie and Patch all arrived right after her – with Jane, Chloe and Bev on top of them. Kyra hadn't bolted, she'd gone to get help!

Jane, Chloe and Bev jumped down the instant they landed and ran towards me.

'Quick... hold hands!' Jane cried out.

Chloe got to me first and hauled me up onto my feet with one hand, then Bev grabbed her other hand and I reached out for Jane's.

I felt a shiver run through me as Bev grabbed Jane's other hand and completed the circle.

'Munimentum!' Uttered Jane, so intensely that the word seemed almost solid.

Lightning bolts crackled from the wands all around us, but their bolts just bounced up into the sky or kicked holes in the sand, none of them got through to us.

I caught a flicker in the corner of my eye and saw Seefa shrink back to her cat form and streak away out of the menage. Thank god!

The wicches stood and glared at our circle.

Beatrice pushed through to the front. 'So, Jane... are you still protecting your abomination?'

I was getting fed up with being called an abomination.

'You can't have her!' Jane hissed.

'She must be banished once more,' Beatrice announced theatrically. 'The world cannot return to what it once was.'

The wicches of the Grand Coven nodded and murmured agreement. But to me it seemed like Beatrice was reading from a script... saying what they all wanted to hear, but not quite meaning it.

She waved her wand. 'I command you to give her to me!'

Jane smiled. 'I am no longer in your thrall, Beatrice. I don't know how long you've been clouding my mind, but it is clouded no more.'

Beatrice's face creased in sudden anger. 'You broke the bond?' Her eyes slitted. 'But no matter. I command you, Cassiopeia, to come to me!'

She turned her gaze my way, and her eyes widened, like they were trying to bore through the back of my head.

'I said... Come to me! You at least are still in my thrall. You cannot disobey!'

Jane glanced sideways at me. 'Do you feel anything?'

I shrugged. 'I don't think so.'

Then Jane smiled and looked back to Beatrice. 'I think that proves Cassiopea's spirit is not inside Poppy!'

What? Did Jane mean that? Was I really just me?

'But...' Stuttered Beatrice. 'Her spirit was returned here, to settle where it may, within the most vulnerable girl-child. How can this girl not be she, who Kyra chose for her rider, and who Lucifer has protected?'

Quiet words from behind Beatrice stopped her in mid-sentence.

'You called me... I'm here.'

That voice! No...

My head spun to search for the owner of the voice at the same time as everyone else. And there, standing close to the wagon, looking tiny against its huge wheels, stood little Kate.

'Cassiopeia,' murmured Beatrice. Not an accusation this time, more a greeting to a long-lost sister.

'Who?' Kate's tiny voice whimpered. She was wearing her stable gear and her whole body was shaking.

'You!' Beatrice waved her wand at the creature up on the wagon. 'Throw her in the cage.'

The ugly creature didn't hesitate, it just flopped down to the ground with a weird, ungainly grace, then loped towards the back of the wagon, scooping up Kate on the way.

'No!' I went to run to help Kate, but Chloe and Jane held my hands tight.

'Don't break the circle,' Jane hissed. 'It's our only protection.'

'But we can't let them take her.'

A scream cut through the air and suddenly Kate's mum appeared, clambering over the menage gate and running at the creature as it reached the back of the wagon. She wrapped her arms around Kate and tried to wrestle her from the creature's hold. Her feet left the ground and her shoes flew off as the creature swung Kate left then right to shake her off.

But her hold on Kate was as strong as a mother's love. She would not let go.

'Throw them both in!' Yelled Beatrice.

And an instant later the creature had tossed them into back of the wagon. They slid and rolled as they hit the floor of the cage and the gate slammed shut behind them.

'Now follow me!' Beatrice turned her horse, galloped down the clear centre of the menage and leapt into the sky.

The ugly creature bounced and loped to the front of the wagon, jumped up into the driver's seat, and cracked a whip over the team of horses. They skidded around and thundered after Beatrice.

There was nothing we could do but watch as the team of horses leapt into the sky dragging the heavy wagon after them.

Some of the wicches in the menage ran to their horses and leapt into the air to follow the wagon, but most stayed where they were, looking around at each other.

Jane kept a tight hold on our hands. 'Keep the circle, girls.'

The wicches that were left didn't seem much of a threat, and milled around in confusion muttering to each other.

'Who's in charge here?' Jane called out in her loud menage-voice.

There was a lot more milling and glancing around until finally a bent, old figure huffed out, 'For goodness' sake!' And hobbled over towards our circle.

Despite the lines on her face, her eyes were piercing blue.

'No one, that's the answer!' She cackled. 'Our esteemed leader and her whole *senior management team* have just flown off.'

She said *senior management team* like it was something nasty she'd just stepped in.

'In direct contravention of rule 20.07 part 3, I might add, that expressly forbids flying during the hours of daylight,' she went on.

Behind her there were a lot of outraged murmurs that sounded like agreement.

'Do you still mean us harm?' Jane asked.

The bent figure glanced behind her at the rest of the wicches, then back to Jane. 'You are Janicus, respected by the whole wicche community... and these three girls are precious, the first new coven in a hundred years. And since it turns out none of you are Cassiopeia reincarnated, then of course we mean you no harm.'

The mutters behind her sounded like agreement and there was a lot of nodding of heads.

'Thankyou Wilnetta, your wisdom as always is inarguable.'

It seemed Jane knew this old wicche.

The bent figure kept on mumbling to herself rather than acknowledge Jane's compliment. 'If that Beatrice was still here, or any of her *senior management team*, I might mean them a bit of harm, though.'

Jane relaxed and let go of my hand, and the tingling drained away and with it the strength in my legs. I sank to the ground and sat down, and saw Chloe and Bev do the same.

The bent old wicche was still muttering. 'Always ordering us around. Acting like they're something *special*. Who made them *senior*, that's what I'd like to know.'

Guilt was wringing me out inside. How could I feel so elated? Just because I wasn't about to be taken over by an evil spirit, when Jane and her mum had paid the price for that and been dragged away in a cage.

'What about Kate and her mum?' I asked Jane. 'If she's taking them to Woolly Hole, we've got to stop her.'

Jane looked down at me and shook her head. 'We'd never catch up with them, Poppy. The horses, you girls, me, we're all too tired. And even if we did catch them, we'd have no way of protecting ourselves.'

She gazed up into the sky. 'And on top of all that, I'm not even sure that's where they're going.'

19

Back to the Hole

Mum was shocked when I asked her if she'd take me on a geography field trip.

'But you haven't even started at your new school yet.'

'I know, but Chloe and Bev were meant to do it as homework during the summer break, and they didn't, and now it's the last week of the holidays... and if I did it with them, I'd be hitting the ground running in my new school.'

Mum stared at me over her breakfast cornflakes, trying to take it all in. 'I suppose I could take a day off, where do you need to go?'

'Woolly Hole.'

'But that's... miles away.'

I showed her my phone. 'It's just a five-hour drive on Google.'

'Five hours? We'd have to start first thing... and even then, we wouldn't be back 'til really late.'

'Thanks mum.'

'I don't think I've agreed yet.'

'Can we go tomorrow?'

Mum was right. It was a long way by car. We picked up Chloe and Bev from their houses at six in the morning the next day, but what with stopping for the loo and getting food, we still didn't arrive there until gone twelve.

It was strange, parking in the carpark at the caves when it was nearly full up. Last time we'd been here it had been dark and deserted.

Mum led us to the ticket office and booked us on the next tour at one o'clock in the afternoon. That gave us time to take a look around the gift shop and also ring Jane.

'We're here,' I whispered into my phone, standing outside while Chloe and Bev got some sweets to keep us going, and while mum was in the loo.

'Great. But remember, be careful.'

'There's tons of people here,' I assured Jane. 'Gotta go.'

I put my phone in my pocket as I saw mum come out through the gift shop door. 'Come on, Poppy, the tour's about to start.'

'The cave system is over twenty miles in length adding all of the passageways together,' a spotty, gangly teenager was announcing to us all. The one o'clock tour group was in a holding room before we entered the main tunnel into the cave system.

'And a funny fact you might not know... these caves are called Woolly Hole after the sheep that discovered them. Nearly fifty years ago a local farmer was looking for his favourite sheep and heard bleating coming from a crevice in the ground. Then, when he made his way down to rescue her, he discovered the cave system we now know as Woolly Hole.'

A child at the front held up a hand. 'So, was his sheep called Woolly?'

The teenager looked down. 'Yes, the farmer had indeed named her Woolly.'

We were at the back and Chloe snorted a laugh. 'Wonder if he had a chicken called Feathery?'

'Or a cat called Furry?' Added Bev.

'Or, I don't know, a tortoise called Shelley?'

Mum gave us a glare as we dissolved into giggles. 'Isn't this meant to be your field trip?'

Then the teenager opened a doorway and took us through into the main tunnel.

Lamps on the walls washed light upwards and downwards, making it all seem very different from when we'd sneaked through here with just Jane's lantern and the flashlights on our phones.

As the group wandered through the caves it strung out, only bunching up when the teenager stopped and spouted more interesting facts about a particular wall, or stalactite, or view through a hole. I motioned to the others to hold back, and we let mum get ahead of us.

'Is that it?' Bev suddenly whispered.

We were going past a side tunnel that had a length of yellow tape across it and a sign saying, 'No public access.'

I wasn't sure. 'I don't remember the tape.'

Then Chloe said, 'I think this is it.'

We stopped and let the stragglers at the back of the group wander past us.

Then we got our phones out and switched on their flashlights and ducked under the tape.

'Be careful,' muttered Bev. 'If this isn't the right tunnel, there might be another hole or something.'

Chloe had taken the lead and was walking quickly, the white light from her phone making stark shadows slide across the rough walls.

Then light started coming from up ahead. Swirling yellows and blues and greens and reds that washed along the floor and walls and got brighter as we went.

This was definitely the right tunnel.

It ended at the huge cavern that I remembered so well from last time we were here, and from a bunch of nightmares I'd had since.

Flat rock surrounded a gaping hole in the middle, and out of the hole a tornado of coloured light circled up and out towards the rocky roof above us.

'That's not magic being sucked back in, is it?' Muttered Chloe.

'No, that's it still coming out,' agreed Bev.

I stared at the tornado. If I threw myself into it, would it hold me up... like it had in Bev's illusion?

'So, it's like Jane said,' I whispered.

'Yeah,' agreed Chloe. 'They didn't bring Kate here.'

Which meant Kate, and her mum, were still okay. If you call being prisoners of an evil wicche being okay. 'Come on, we'd better get back to the group.'

I held up my phone and led the way back out towards the main tunnels of the caves again.

On the drive back we were all quiet.

Mum was great, she didn't complain once about the driving... although we did have to stop four times for her to grab coffees.

In the dark I watched the signs and motorway bridges and embankments at the side of the road flash by.

I felt a familiar twist of guilt inside my tummy; I should be shocked and devasted that Beatrice hadn't banished Cassiopeia, and that magic was still pouring back into the world; and scared to death that the evil spirit of Cassiopeia might rise again.

But instead I was excited.

I was a wicche. Part of the first new coven for one hundred years.

I didn't know what it meant for our world that magic was coming back into it, not now there were mobile phones, and the internet, and jet planes, and cars.

And if pixies were already back... did that mean all those other mythical animals... fairies, elves, demons, vampires, trolls... even dragons... wouldn't be far behind?

There were only a few things I knew for sure.

I had two new sisters that I could rely on no matter what.

We could all do magic, which *had* to put us ahead of the curve.

And... I was starting at my new school next week.

THE END

Printed in Great Britain
by Amazon